Sally Bradford

THE STORY OF A REBEL GIRL

by Dorothy and Thomas Hoobler
in conjunction with Carey-Greenberg Associates
illustrations by Robert Gantt Steele

SILVER BURDETT PRESS
Parsippany, New Jersey

Published by Silver Burdett Press
A Division of Simon & Schuster
229 Jefferson Road, Parsippany, New Jersey 07054

Designed by JP Design Associates

Manufactured in the United States of America
ISBN 0-382-39258-2 (LSB) 10 9 8 7 6 5 4 3 2 1
ISBN 0-382-39259-0 (PBK) 10 9 8 7 6 5 4 3 2 1

Library of Congress Cataloging-in-Publication Data
Hoobler, Dorothy.
Sally Bradford: The Story of a Rebel Girl/by Dorothy and
Thomas Hoobler. Carey-Greenberg Associates: illustrated by
Robert Gantt Steele.
p. cm. (Her Story)
Summary: A young girl experiences the cruelty, danger, and
destruction of the Civil War in Virginia.
1. United States–History–Civil War, 1861-1865–Juvenile fiction.
[1United States–History–Civil War, 1861-1865–Fiction.] I. Hoobler,
Thomas. II. Steele, Robert Gantt, ill. III. Carey-Greenberg Associates.
IV. Title. V. Series.
PZ7.H76227Sal   1996
[Fic]–dc20   96-16047   CIP   AC

Photo credits: Photo research: Po-Yee McKenna; 120,© Brown Brothers;
121, top: © Culiver Pictures, Inc., bottom: © Culiver Pictures, Inc.;120-121,
© THE GRANGER COLLECTION, New York.

CURR
PZ
7
.H76227
Sal
1997

Table of Contents

Chapter 1
A New Nation

Sally Bradford remembered that spring day in April 1861 all her life. The frost had gone out of the ground, and Sally was turning over the soil in the garden to get it ready for planting. Her brother Tim was supposed to help. But as usual Tim had wandered off, looking for a wild turkey that he heard gobbling down by the creek.

Sally didn't mind. She was glad that spring had come at last. Everyone was tired of eating the dried-up turnips and carrots and potatoes from the root cellar. Even the preserved fruits and vegetables, which had been put up in jars last fall, were starting to taste old. Winter had been unusually long in the Tidewater country of Virginia, where the Bradfords' farm was. But in less than a month there would be fresh lettuce, radishes, and green onions on the table. The first young chickens would soon be baking in the oven on

Sunday afternoon.

Even the bees knew it was spring. They buzzed past Sally, looking for the new yellow blossoms of forsythia and dandelions. In a little while, Sally's father could take new honey from the wooden-frame hives that stood near the garden. Sally's mouth watered as she thought of the way it would taste on one of her mother's fresh-baked biscuits.

And then the sound of hoofbeats came hammering down the road. Sally looked up as her brother Rob galloped through the gate on his chestnut stallion, Champ. Seeing Sally, Rob waved his hat and shouted, "It's happened! Virginia's seceded!"

He jumped down and swept Sally off her feet, twirling her around. "We're part of a new country now, Sally. The Confederate States of America!" Before he put her down Timmy was there too, shouting "Hoorah for the Confederacy!" Wherever he'd been hiding, it hadn't been far.

All the uproar brought the other Bradfords to hear the news. Papa and Gramp ran up from the barn, and Mama and Nora, Sally's older sister, came out onto the porch, their hands dusty with flour.

Rob told the tale proudly. He had ridden into Yorktown that morning, eager to learn if Virginia would join the seven other states that had already declared their independence.

"There was a big crowd in front of the courthouse," Rob said. "People were telling stories about what they heard, but you could see nobody really knew anything. Then Judge Sutherland came out on the courthouse steps. He said he'd just gotten a telegraph message from Richmond. Everyone got real quiet. Then he told us. The Virginia legislature had voted to secede from the United States and join the Confederacy."

"I knew it," Gramp said. "Lincoln made a big mistake when he said he'd send the army to put down the rebellion. After that, Virginia had to join the rest of the southern states. That's where we belong."

Rob nodded. "Everybody said so. 'Cept for a few who said it'd mean war."

"Why, of course there'll be a war," Gramp said. "But it won't last long. I fought in the War of 1812, boy. And I wasn't any older than you."

Sally smiled. They had heard Gramp's war stories lots of times.

"This'll be easier than that," Gramp said. "Lincoln can't raise an army big enough to conquer the South."

"That's what Judge Sutherland told us," said Rob. "He said if we showed we'd fight for our rights, Lincoln would have to back down." Rob looked away and took a deep breath. Sally saw that he had something else to tell, that he was a little afraid of saying. "Well, comes to it," Rob said, "the judge asked for volunteers to raise a company of soldiers."

Papa and Mama glanced at each other. Papa put his hand on Rob's shoulder. "And what did you do?"

Rob shrugged. "Well, I signed up. Most all the young fellows did."

Mama put her hand over her mouth. "Rob, you're just a boy!"

Sally didn't say anything, but she didn't think Mama was right. At seventeen, Rob was taller than Father. He rode a horse as fast as anybody could, and he'd won the wrestling contest at the church picnic last summer.

Gramp stepped up and shook Rob's hand. "I'm proud of you, boy. You did the right thing!" Rob grinned.

"How old do you have to be?" Tim piped up. Mama gave him a swat. "You hush. You're barely 12."

"When is all this going to happen?" Papa asked.

"Not right away," said Rob. "There's going to be a big rally tonight, though."

"I guess we'll have to go into town and see it," Papa said.

So after dinner the Bradfords hitched up their wagon, just as they did every Sunday for church. While they were getting ready upstairs, Sally noticed that Nora tried on three dresses before she decided on the one she liked best. Sally knew why. Nora expected to see Jack Wilkins, a friend of Rob's that Nora was sweet on.

They could hear the noise from the town even before they got there. It was like the Fourth of July, only bigger. Bands were playing and people were singing. Crowds of people were marching through the streets waving the new flag of the Confederacy. Men were shooting pistols into the air.

Sally jumped down from the wagon when she saw her friend Janie, who lived in town. "Did Rob sign up for the army?" Janie asked.

"He sure did," said Sally.

"Good thing too," Janie said. "There were some boys who didn't, at first." She giggled. "I heard that their girlfriends sent them petticoats to shame them into joining. If I was a boy, I'd go to fight. Wouldn't you?"

"I guess," Sally said. "But Mama didn't like it when Rob told her."

"She'll get over it," said Janie. "And anyway, the war won't last long."

That's what everybody thought. Rob and Jack Wilkins and all the other young men seemed like heroes. They stood on the courthouse steps while the judge and the mayor and the minister gave speeches.

5

People cheered and the band played. And afterward, Sally saw Nora walk off arm-in-arm with Jack.

It started to get late, but nobody was ready to go home. After Sally got tired of all the celebrating, she went back to the wagon and stretched out. She must have fallen asleep, because the next thing she knew, Papa and Mama were talking quietly in the darkness. They hadn't noticed her.

"I talked to Judge Sutherland," Papa said. "Told him I thought Rob was a little young."

"Rob doesn't have any idea what war is like," Mama said.

"I guess none of us does," said Papa. "But the judge said that they needed some of the older men too. To lead the boys. He asked me if I wanted to be one of officers in the company. I didn't want to tell him yes till I talked with you."

There was a long silence. Finally Mama said, "You want to go, don't you?"

Papa's voice was husky. "It...well, it's my duty, I guess. I don't think the boys ought to be the only ones to fight. But then you and Tim and the girls will have to do a lot more of the farm work."

This time Mama spoke so softly that Sally had to strain to hear. "The work doesn't bother me. You just make sure you keep Rob safe. And...and you better come back to me yourself, Will Bradford."

6

"Mary, I'll think of you and the children all the time. Don't fret. We'll be back by harvest time, for sure."

"May the Lord watch over you," Mama said.

So for the next two weeks Sally helped her mother sew uniforms for Rob and Papa. Tim promised to plant the garden, but instead he spent most of his time watching the soldiers in town. Nora clipped off a lock of her pretty blond hair and put it in a locket for Jack Wilkins to carry.

That gave Sally the idea to make something for Rob too. She cut cloth from a couple of old dresses in the attic and made him a sash with the red and blue of the Confederate flag. She sewed his initials on it, and gave it to him on the day he and Papa left.

Rob wound the sash around his waist and then gave Sally a kiss on the cheek. She felt so proud that she started to cry. "Stop that now," Rob said. "I'm going to be the best-looking soldier in the army because of you."

He and Papa did look wonderful as they went down the road. Because Papa was an officer, he was allowed to take a horse. So Champ went off to war too.

Papa bent down to give Mama a last kiss. Mama squeezed his hand as if she would never let go. Sally watched her mother force a smile, so she did too. It was wonderful and sad at the same time.

But that evening at dinner, the sadness took over. Though Gramp and Tim talked excitedly about the war, nothing could hide the fact that there were two empty places at the table. Mama kept going out to the kitchen, and Sally knew what she was thinking. How long would it be before Papa and Rob sat down to dinner with them again?

Chapter 2

Hard Work

Everyone chipped in to do the work Papa and Rob would have done. Sally and Tim helped Gramp plant the corn. Nora volunteered to milk the cows, but she complained that her hands and back ached at the end of the day.

By the end of May, the spring vegetables finally did get planted. Mama's rosebushes in front of the porch started to open their buds. Even the corn plants had sprouted the first set of green leaves.

Each afternoon, they waited eagerly for the post-man's wagon to pass by. The day the first letter from Papa arrived, the Bradfords read it so many times that the paper started to wear out. He and Rob were at a camp near Richmond. The food wasn't as good as Mama's cooking. All the soldiers did was drill all day long and learn to follow orders, so they could stay together if there was a battle. Papa wrote that he loved them all and expected to be home soon.

Of course Mama was glad that there hadn't been any battles yet. After dinner, Gramp read aloud the war stories from the Richmond newspaper. There wasn't much real news, because both the North and the South were still trying to get their armies ready.

"Lincoln asked Robert E. Lee to be the head of the Union army," Gramp told them. "But Bobby Lee is a true Virginian. He chose to fight for his country, the Confederate States of America. Just like his daddy and uncle, who had fought in the *first* War of Independence. The one when we beat the British. Now we've got to fight the North. With Bobby Lee on our side, we can't lose. Lincoln hasn't got a general like him."

The work on the farm was harder than Sally thought it would be. She went out every day with a hoe to weed between the corn rows. As the days grew warmer, she had to wear a bonnet to keep her face from being sunburned. But the bonnet itched and her hands were covered with blisters. At night she had to soak them in cool water.

Mama told her to take a day off from the hoeing. "I've got another chore for you," she told Sally. "Take two or three jars of honey over to the Mallorys. I think their cook will trade us a half pound of tea for it."

"Why don't I just go into town and buy tea?" Sally asked.

"It's too expensive right now," Mama said. "Those confounded Yankees have started a blockade."

"What's a blockade?"

"It means that their navy is stopping ships from landing at southern ports. The Yankees are trying to stop the Confederacy from getting the supplies it needs to fight the war."

"But why would they want to stop us from having tea?"

"Oh, they're trying to stop everything they can. Sugar, farm tools, even thread." Mama laughed. "I guess they think we'll give up if they annoy us enough."

"That won't work," said Sally. "We'll always have enough food, anyway."

"I'm sure we will," said Mama.

Sally saddled up Jake, the old horse that she had learned to ride on. He was too old to pull a plow now, but he didn't mind carrying her and Tim around. She gave him one of the stale carrots from the root cellar. "Pretty soon we'll have fresh carrots, Jake," she said, as he took it from her hand. "I'll make sure you get one."

The Mallorys owned a big tobacco plantation

just down the road. As Sally rode along, she saw some of the Mallorys' slaves working in the fields. An overseer on a horse cracked his whip whenever one of them stopped too long to rest. It was well known that Mr. Mallory worked his slaves hard.

Papa had always declared he would never have a slave. Sally had heard him say, "I just don't think it's right to keep another human in bondage." She knew Papa hadn't gone to war to fight for slavery. But like most of their neighbors, he believed that Virginia had a right to be part of a new country if it wanted to.

Mr. Mallory himself hadn't enlisted in the Confederate army. Sally thought that wasn't fair. But the Confederate government said that slaveowners should stay at home to keep their slaves under control. There were always a lot of rumors that if the Yankees invaded the South, the slaves would rise up to join them.

As far as Sally could see, there was no danger of that. The Mallorys' slaves looked pretty friendly whenever she saw them. In fact, the Mallorys' cook Celia was a slave, and so were all the servants in the Mallorys' big house.

Nobody could ever be afraid of Celia. She was out in the yard plucking chickens when Sally rode up on Jake. Celia was a tall woman who always had a smile for everybody. "Hey, there!" she called, as Sally dismounted. "I see you brought some of that nice honey. Hope it's for us."

"Mama wanted to see if you would trade it for half a pound of tea," Sally said.

"Oh, tea, yes. We're swimmin' in tea," Celia said with a laugh. "But I'd rather drink coffee any day. Miz Mallory is the only one who likes tea, and she drinks just one or two cups a day. She'll be pleased when I mix a little of this honey with it. Take it on inside. Tell that girl to scoop out as much tea as you like."

The kitchen smelled even better than the Bradfords' did on baking day. A slave girl about Tim's age was stirring a big pot of stew. She looked up. "Who're you?" she asked.

"I'm Sally. I brought some honey."

The girl shrugged. Her bony shoulders showed right through the thin gray dress she wore.

"You look like you could use some of that stew," Sally said.

"I never took none," the girl said quickly.

"I didn't mean you did." As Sally set the jars of honey down on a table, the girl's big eyes followed her.

"I had some honey one time," the girl said. "But the bees stung me when I took it. How'd you gather so much of it?"

Sally told her about the wooden hives that had trays so you could take the extra honey without disturbing the bees. "You could have a spoonful if you like," Sally said.

The girl looked at her suspiciously. "You won't tell?"

"I promise," said Sally. She lifted the wax top off one of the jars. Quick as a flash, the girl dipped her fingers inside and then stuck them into her mouth. "Mmm," she said. "That's good, all right."

"Celia said you'd give me some tea," Sally said.

"Tea's in the cupboard over there," the girl said. "Put it in one of the empty tins."

Sally wasn't sure how much half a pound was, so she filled one of the tins with tea. Nobody seemed to mind anyway. The girl had gone back to stirring the stew.

"Is Celia your mother?" Sally asked.

The girl shook her head. "Master done sold my mamma."

"Oh. I'm sorry," said Sally. "I guess you miss her."

"Sometimes I do," the girl said. "But now I get to work here in the big house, so Celia says I'm lucky. 'Cause I don't have to be out in the fields."

"She's right," Sally said. "I have to hoe the weeds, and look at what it did to my hands."

14

The girl looked at Sally's blisters. She seemed surprised. "Don't you have no slaves to do that?" she asked.

"No. And Papa and my brother Rob went off to the war, so we have to take their places."

"Why'd they go to war then?"

"Well, because … it was their duty."

The girl looked around to see if anybody else was listening. "Is it true there's a man named Lincoln who wants to free the slaves?"

"That's right," said Sally.

"If I was free, know what I'd do? I'd go see if I could find my mamma."

Sally nodded. "I guess I'd do the same."

"What'd you say your name was?" the girl asked.

"Sally."

"Mine's Mattie. I hope your pa don't get killed."

Sally bit her lip. "I hope you find your mamma someday too, Mattie."

"Don't tell 'bout that honey, remember?"

"I won't."

Outside, Celia was still plucking chickens. "You get all the tea you needed?" she said.

"Oh yes, thank you, Celia."

"That Mattie didn't give you any bother?"

"No, no."

"Sometimes she's too free with her tongue. But she'll learn. You come back with honey anytime, hear? And tell your mamma that we could always use butter too."

"I will."

Sally rode home on Jake slowly, taking another look at the slaves working in Mr. Mallory's field. Most slaves that Sally had ever talked to seemed happy, like Celia. But they were usually servants who worked inside the house. Nobody used a whip on them.

Sally was glad she had given Mattie the honey. Thinking about what the girl had said, Sally smiled to herself. One thing she was sure of–if she was Mr. Mallory, she wouldn't let Mattie cook dinner. Not after selling her mother away.

Chapter 3
War News

Gramp was excited. He waved a newspaper at Sally as she brought a basket of green beans into the kitchen. "We beat 'em!" Gramp shouted. "We licked the Yankees!"

Sally dropped the basket. She didn't know whether to shout or cry. It was mid-July, and she felt like a chicken that had been left in the oven too long. There seemed to be no end to the work that had to be done.

"Is the war over?" she asked. "Will Papa and Rob be home soon?"

"I don't know," Gramp said. "There's only a little bit here in the paper. It says there was a big battle at Manassas two days ago. It was the first time the Yankees tried to march down into Virginia. And our boys sent 'em running all the way back to Washington."

They learned more about the battle the next day. Gramp went into town, where messages from Richmond were posted in the window of the telegraph office. When he came back, the rest of the family gathered to hear the war news.

It was true. The Confederate army had won a battle at the town of Manassas, near a little stream called Bull Run. But the cost had been high.

"They say there were more than two thousand men killed or wounded on both sides," Gramp told them.

"Two thousand?" said Mama. "That seems like so many. Do they… have any names?"

Gramp shook his head. "Too early. When you have a battle like that, it's a mess." He lit his pipe and nodded his head, remembering what it had been like in the War of 1812.

"First thing is to tend to the wounded," Gramp said. "Those that are worst off will be carried on wagons to the hospital in Richmond. And then the dead have to be buried. The officers are supposed to make a list of them, but it'll be days before we find out who they are."

They all looked at each other. Sally knew everybody was thinking the same thing: What if Papa or Rob had been killed?

"We can pray," Mama said. "That's all we can

do." Sally took her hand and squeezed it. "Don't worry, Mama."

Sunday they went into town for church. That day the list of those who had fallen in battle started to come over the telegraph. Reverend Walker read the names from the pulpit. There were many that nobody knew. But whenever he came to a familiar name, people in the church screamed.

The list was long. It took half an hour for Reverend Walker to read all of it. Sally closed her eyes with each name, hoping that it wouldn't be Papa or Rob. Finally it was over. No Will Bradford. No Rob Bradford.

Sally was so relieved. But as they left the church, she saw the weeping families whose loved ones had been on the list. Mama went over to comfort Mrs. Breen, whose son Pat had been reported killed. There were six men killed or wounded, just from their town. And in other towns, more than two thousand more. It was hard to imagine.

On the way home, Sally asked Gramp, "Will the war end now?"

"Hard to say. Prob'ly not. One victory generally isn't enough to stop a war. Lincoln is said to be a mighty stubborn man."

Three days later, they finally got a letter. It was from Rob. Mama's hands shook as she opened it.

Everyone gathered around the dining table to listen as she read it aloud.

"I guess you heard by now there was a battle," Rob wrote. "Don't worry about us. We're fine, but Pa's busy with all the things the officers have to do. So he told me to write.

"I never saw such a thing as this battle before. There was so much confusion you could hardly tell what was happening. The officers yell at you to go first this way, and then that. We more or less got into a long line. I couldn't see to either end of it. You can't imagine how many men there were. I never saw so many.

"Anyways, pretty soon the Yankee army showed up. People started to fire at 'em right away, but that was dumb. Couldn't hit anybody from that far off.

"The Yankees looked like they were having as much trouble staying in line as we were. But way off to our left, a whole lot of 'em charged forward. That was the start of everything. We heard the order to fire our rifles, and commenced. You couldn't tell if you hit anybody. You just fired.

"Pretty soon we started hearing the Yankee bullets fly by us. They sounded just like a swarm of bees, truth. In fact, I kept telling myself they were only bees, so I wouldn't get afraid. I kept firing, but by now there was so much smoke you couldn't see to aim. People all around us were screaming, either because they got hit or because they was just afraid.

"I have to tell you, a lot of men couldn't take it, especially after they saw others fall wounded and bleeding. A bunch down to our left turned and ran. The officers used their swords to try to beat them back into place. But it looked like the Yankees were going to break through that part of the line.

"Then one of the most amazing things happened. One of the officers on our left pointed up to where we were. Our general had pretty much kept us all together. He stood up right in the thick of the fighting, and all of us took courage from that. His name is Thomas Jackson. This other officer shouted, 'Look there at Jackson, standing like a stone wall! Rally behind the Virginians.'

"And would you believe, they did. After that, everything went in our favor. Our line held fast, and then the Yankees finally turned away. All we could see were the backs of them heading back the way they had come. A big cheer went up on our side. I wish you could've heard it.

"Well, there's still lots to do now. I have to close. Pa and I send our love."

Mama passed the letter around the table so they all could read it. Tears were streaming down her face. "Mama, don't cry," Sally said. "Rob was so brave.

And he's safe."

"I know," said Mama. "But he doesn't even realize...." She shook her head.

"He stood up like a man," Gramp said admiringly.

"Oh, I wish I'd been there," Tim said. "You know, I hear the army has drummer boys as young as me."

And by the next day, somehow Tim had gotten himself a drum. He stood out in the garden by the beehives, beating it. "Tim," Sally told him, "you're driving us all crazy with that noise."

"I'm trying to stir up the bees," Tim said. "So I'll know what it's like to be shot at."

"You'd be helping a lot more if you did some of the chores. Mama and Nora are making bandages to send to Richmond for the wounded."

"I don't know how to do that. I want to go and fight!"

Sally looked at him. Now she knew why Mama had cried over Rob's letter. He made war sound like fun.

Chapter 4
Right or Wrong?

It was nearly spring again. A year had gone by, and the war still had not ended. Papa and Rob wrote letters often, but they had not had to fight another battle. Gramp read the family news about other battles in the West, along the Mississippi River. But that seemed far away.

Without Papa and Rob to help, the corn harvest had been skimpy. They used most of it to feed the chickens and cows. Christmas of 1861 had been a bleak one. Because the northern navy's blockade had tightened, sugar was now very scarce. So Mama made pies with the honey, but they didn't taste the same.

In early March of 1862, Sally's mother sent her on another errand to the Mallorys. "We've run out of thread," Mama said, "and the stores in town don't have any. Take some butter and see if they'll give you thread for it. Tea too, if they can spare it."

"Will the Mallorys have some?" Sally asked.

Mama sighed. "They're a rich family. If you have enough money, you can always find the things you need. The Mallorys must have enough thread and cloth to make dresses and shirts for their slaves."

After Sally wrapped the butter in cheesecloth, she thought about Mattie. She hadn't seen the slave girl since autumn, the last time Sally had delivered honey. Sally had started bringing Mattie a little honey each time. Mattie enjoyed it so much that Sally didn't want to disappoint her. So she filled a small jar from the little that was left in the cellar. There wouldn't be any more till spring. But that would come soon.

The road was muddy, for a cold rain had fallen the past two days. Old Jake seemed to enjoy the sloppy ride, however. Maybe the cool mud was good for his hooves.

There weren't any slaves working in the Mallorys' fields today. It wasn't time to plant tobacco yet. Sally saw a few slaves down by their cabins at the far end of the plantation. They were sawing up pine logs for firewood. A few wisps of smoke wafted from the chimneys of the cabins.

Up at the kitchen for the big house, she tied Jake's bridle to a post and went inside. It smelled good here, as always. Turkey was roasting, and two freshly made pies stood cooling on a counter. I'll bet they have sugar in them, Sally thought.

But Mattie wasn't there. A new girl had taken her place. "Where's Mattie?" Sally asked her. The girl just looked at her and shook her head.

"Is Celia here?" Sally asked. The girl pointed to a door that led to the pantry. Sally went through and found Celia slicing a ham. "My!" Celia said. "Did you bring me somethin' good today?"

"Butter," Sally said.

"Mmm. That's one thing the Yankees can't keep out of here, long as we have cows in Virginia. And what do you need for it?"

Sally took a deep breath. "Just about everything. Sugar, tea, thread, and maybe a few slices of that ham."

Celia chuckled. "My oh my, girl. I'd be in trouble if I gave you all that. Miz Mallory'd send me down to the cabins with Mattie."

"With Mattie? Why is she down at the cabins?"

"Well, see, she dropped a dish of gravy when she was serving it. Broke it and made a mess on the carpet." She shook her head. "I told that girl to be careful. Miz Mallory had her whipped."

"Whipped?" Sally was horrified.

Celia lowered her voice. "Miz Mallory was having one of her headaches that day. But anyway, you didn't come to hear about that. I'll go on to the house and see about the thread and ask if we can spare the rest."

As Sally waited, she felt her hands shaking. She knew slaves were whipped, but she thought it was for something terrible. Why would anyone whip a girl just for breaking a dish?

Pretty soon Celia returned with two spools of thread. "Miz Mallory said she could spare these, and you could have a couple scoops of sugar and two slices of ham. But no tea. Miz Mallory likes her tea, and it's scarce now, you know."

Sally could see three big tins of tea on the pantry shelves but didn't say anything.

"Miz Mallory said if you had some more honey, she'd trade you tea for it," Celia said.

Sally hesitated for a second. "No. There won't be any more honey till the spring."

"I was afraid so." Celia winked. "Well, I'll make the slices of ham extra thick. But bring some honey as soon as the bees wake up."

As Sally put the bundle of food in her saddlebag, she felt guilty for not trading the honey for tea. She hoped Mama wouldn't mind not having tea.

Sally had something else in mind for the honey. When she reached the little path that led down to the slave cabins, she looked around. Nobody could see her, and she headed Jake down the path. He shook his head as if to warn her this was the wrong way. But she tapped her feet on his sides, and he went on.

Down by the cabins, a slave, who was cutting wood, walked over to meet her. He was gray-haired and his face was deeply lined. "You're in the wrong place, miss," he said.

"I'm looking for Mattie," she said.

The man frowned. "No one named Mattie here," he said. Though he was still polite, his voice had deepened. Sally was just a little afraid, but she forced herself to say, "I have something to give her. I know she's here. Please tell me where."

He shook his head. "Mr. Mallory wouldn't like you here at all."

"Well, he won't whip *me*," she said angrily.

The corners of the man's mouth went up a little. "Guess not. Look in the last cabin in the row. I'll hold your horse."

As she dismounted, he added, "But be quick, miss. *I* could get in trouble."

She understood, and hurried down the row. Sally had never been in a slave cabin before. Opening the door, she saw that there were several women and children sitting on the floor. They all stopped talking and stared at her.

"Is Mattie here?" she asked.

No one answered. "My name is Sally," she

explained. "I have something for her."

"Over here," came a muffled voice. The people moved aside to let Sally past. She saw Mattie lying face down on a straw mattress. An older woman was rubbing grease on her skin.

Sally gasped when she saw the ugly welts across Mattie's back. Mattie turned her head to look up at her. "Is that what you wanted to see?" she said angrily.

"Oh no," Sally said. "When I heard ... I mean, I wanted to bring you this honey." She knelt down and took the little jar from her coat pocket.

Mattie sat up, pulling her dress around her. "Oh my. That's what I need right now." She took the jar and scooped a little honey into her mouth. "That's just so good," she said.

Then she looked sharply at Sally. "What'd you do this for?" she asked.

"Because ...." Sally thought, and remembered what her father had said. "Because I don't think people should be kept in bondage. Or whipped."

The others murmured to themselves. "Miss," one of them said. "You got to get out of here. We'll all get whipped if anybody finds you here."

Sally stood up. "I just wanted you to have that," she said to Mattie, and started for the door.

"Wait up," Mattie said. Sally turned.

"I want to be angry at you, you know," Mattie said. The others told her to hush.

Sally was astonished. "Why?" she asked.

"I was just lying here, enjoying myself by hating all white people. I was thinking what I'd do to them if I was free. And then you come along and give me this."

"Not all white people are like the Mallorys," Sally said.

"I guess not," said Mattie. "Let me have your hand."

Sally stepped forward and shyly put her hand in Mattie's. She couldn't remember ever having touched a slave before. Mattie squeezed her hand. "I'll remember," she said. "Get on with you, now."

Sally ran back to Jake, and the gray-haired man gave her the reins as she mounted. "You're a headstrong girl," he said. "Just like Mattie."

"We're friends," Sally said over her shoulder and kicked Jake's sides so that he trotted faster. All the way home, she felt strange, wondering if what she had done was right or wrong.

But she knew she couldn't tell anybody about it. They wouldn't understand. Except Papa. More than anything else, she wanted him to come home so she could tell him. If only the war would stop!

Chapter 5

The Ironclads

The day after Sally brought the honey to Mattie, Tim came home from town with a big smile. "The South is bound to win the war now," he told Sally, who was sweeping the front porch. "It has a ship that can't be sunk."

"What's that?" said Gramp, who had been dozing in his rocking chair in a sunny spot on the porch.

"The South is going to break the Yankee blockade," Tim said, "with a ship that can't be sunk."

Gramp harrumphed. "Hogwash. What kind of ship could that be?"

But in a few days, Gramp read the same story in his newspaper. "It's a new-fangled idea," he told Sally and Tim. "The Confederate navy captured a northern ship called the *Merrimack* at the beginning of the war. It runs on steam, not sail."

Gramp shook his head. They knew he had never

been fond of steamships. "Somebody had the idea to cover it all over with iron plates. Top, sides—the whole thing. The idea is that cannonballs can't hurt it. They call it an ironclad."

"So it can just steam up to the Yankee ships and sink them with its guns," said Tim.

"If it's all covered with iron, how can the sailors see?" Sally asked.

"Portholes, maybe," said Gramp. "Crackpot idea, but I'd like to see this ship for myself. Says here they've renamed it the *Virginia*. It's on the Elizabeth River, at Norfolk."

"Can we take the wagon?" asked Tim.

"I want to go too," Sally said.

"Well," Gramp said, "let's go into town and see if we can find out just exactly where it is."

They told Mama, and she packed them a lunch. "Enjoy yourselves while you can," she said to Sally and Tim. "The spring planting will start soon, and you'll have too much to do then."

When they reached town, there was a big crowd of people in the courthouse square. Everybody was excited. The telegraph had brought the news that the *Virginia* was already in action.

"Yesterday she sank two big Yankee warships," a man told them. "They shot everything they could at her. Even the artillery guns at the Yankee fort on shore. Didn't hurt her one bit."

"I heard the *Virginia* rammed one of the wooden ships and broke it right in two," another said.

"And today it's coming back to clear the rest of the Yankee navy right out of Hampton Roads," added a third.

All at once, everybody had the same idea that Gramp had. People hitched up their wagons, got on their horses, and headed for Hampton Roads. This was the big channel that connected the James River with Chesapeake Bay. For months, not a single Confederate ship had been able to get through there with supplies. The Yankee ships had driven them back.

"We'll have plenty of tea and sugar now," said Sally. "And thread and cloth to make new dresses, and…and Papa and Rob can come home."

"That's right," said Tim. "I guess I'll never get to be a soldier now."

"Not so fast," said Gramp. "We haven't seen this marvel in action yet."

"I wish I'd brought my drum," said Tim.

But plenty of others had. Not only drums, but flutes and bugles and even fiddles. When Sally and Gramp and Tim arrived at Hampton Roads, it sounded like the biggest church picnic in the world. Bands had formed to play "Dixie," the Confederate battle song, and people were singing. Women in their Sunday-best dresses sat on blankets along the bank of the river to watch the *Virginia* steam by. Some had brought their children and babies.

The Bradfords had to leave their wagon and walk through the crowd to find a spot for themselves. Suddenly a big cheer went up and everybody surged forward. Sally was carried along in the crush.

There it was! The first thing Sally thought was that it was about the ugliest thing she'd ever seen. The *Virginia* didn't look like a ship at all. It was like one of the long sheds where farmers hung tobacco to dry. Only it was made entirely of metal that glinted in the sun. Big gun barrels stuck out from ports in its sides. Sally couldn't understand how such a thing could even float.

But the *Virginia* calmly chugged along, leaving a plume of black smoke behind. The only pretty thing about it was the Confederate flag that flew on a staff at the front of the ship. In fact, that was the only way you could tell the front of the ship from the back.

The *Virginia* was heading straight for a wooden sailing ship that was flying the Yankee flag. It was trying to break free from a sandbar where it had run aground. Sally felt sorry for the Yankee ship. With its beautiful white sails filled with wind, it looked like a butterfly about to fight a turtle.

The Yankee ship began to fire its guns. And it was true. They had no effect. She could actually see the cannonballs bounce off the iron sides of the *Virginia*. The *Virginia* didn't even bother to fire back. Tim had moved up next to Sally and said, "It's waiting until it gets so close that its gunners can't miss."

Then a whisper of voices spread through the crowd along the bank. People began to point toward Fort Monroe, the Yankee fort on the other bank of the river. Sally stood on her tiptoes to see. Something else, another odd-looking ship, was coming this way.

The *Virginia* saw it too. It turned away from the sailing ship. Sally realized that inside the metal box, there must be sailors to steer it and fire its guns. She shivered, thinking of what it would be like to be in the darkness inside that ugly ship.

Pretty soon the crowd could see the other strange ship more clearly. Tim realized what it was before anyone else did. "The Yankees have got one too," he shouted. Others murmured that he was right, and it was as if a cold wind had blown down from the north. All the cheerfulness in the crowd suddenly vanished.

The Yankee ship was made of metal too, but it looked completely different from the *Virginia*. It was just a long, flat raft with a round box on top. Sally couldn't help thinking that it looked like a floating hatbox.

Just then blasts of flame shot out from the sides of the box. The sudden roar of the guns caused everyone on the bank to scream.

Again, though, the cannon fire seemed to have no effect on the *Virginia*. It kept chugging toward the other ship, and then slowly, slowly began to turn to one side.

"It's going to fire back," said Tim excitedly, "as soon as its guns are broadside to the other ship."

"But it moves so slowly," Sally said. "The other one can move away."

That was true. When the *Virginia's* guns finally boomed, it looked like they hadn't even hit the hatbox. "They've got to aim at the box on top," somebody said. "There's nothing else to hit."

As the *Virginia's* gunners reloaded, the other ship fired again. The two ships were now so close that the clang of the cannonballs against the metal sides of the *Virginia* echoed across the water.

The Confederate ironclad rocked back and forth from the impact, and Sally feared that it had been damaged. But after a minute, it chugged onward, firing again.

The fight was a strange one. Sally had never seen a naval battle before, but it sounded exciting when Gramp described it. After a while, all this battle seemed to produce was a lot of noise and smoke.

As the two ships circled each other firing their guns, the smoke from their engines made the battle harder to see from the shore. But whenever it cleared, the two ships looked just the same as before.

Once, the *Virginia* seemed to have won. Its guns were firing explosive shells, and one of them struck the hatbox dead on. The fiery blast seemed to go right inside one of the portholes.

As the crowd cheered, the Yankee ironclad drifted off as if everybody inside had been killed. But it wasn't out of action long. If the blast had really killed its pilot, somebody else had taken his place. Once more the ship steamed forward and began to fire its guns.

The crowd sensed that the fight would be a draw. Neither ship could sink, which made it impossible for either to win. Pretty soon the two ironclads just drew away from each other, as if they had run out of ammunition. The *Virginia* headed back to its base in

Norfolk, and the Yankee ship didn't follow.

Disappointed, the crowd began to break up. Someone with a flute tried to start playing "Dixie" again, but no one else joined in. "Let's go home," said Gramp. "Nothing more to see today."

On the trip back, Tim kept talking about the battle and how great the *Virginia* had been. But Gramp didn't say anything for a long time. Then he shook his head. "I guess I'm too old," he said. "Doesn't seem to me that's the way war ought to be. When you can't even see who you're fighting."

"But at least the South hasn't lost," Sally told him. "The Yankees can't make us give up."

"They're going to try," said Gramp. "Lincoln's got a big army. They'll be back down here soon enough."

Chapter 6
The War Arrives

Sally and her family soon learned why the Yankee ironclad, which was called the *Monitor,* had come to Hampton Roads. On a trip to town one Sunday, they listened to a man who had come on horseback from Norfolk. "The Yankees are sending an army by sea down to Fort Monroe," he said. "The *Monitor* is patrolling the bay, keeping the *Virginia* from attacking the Yankee ships."

"How many soldiers?" someone asked.

"Thousands and thousands. I've seen them with my own eyes. All dressed in blue uniforms, carrying their battle gear. There's so many ships arriving that they're lined up in the bay waiting to unload."

The news threw the people of Yorktown into a panic. "They're going to march right up here," somebody shouted. "They'll attack the town." People started talking about what they should do, and Sally heard some saying that they had to get out of the way fast.

A few days later, Gramp showed them on a map what his newspaper said the Yankee plan would be. "Fort Monroe is down here at Chesapeake Bay. After the Yankees land their army, they'll move up the peninsula between the York and James Rivers. They'll head straight toward Richmond." He traced a line on the map with his finger.

"But Gramp," Sally said, "our farm is right where your finger went through."

"Aw, don't worry," said Tim. "Our army will stop the Yankees before they get far."

Gramp shook his head. "Most of the army of Virginia is way up north of here. That's why the Yankees haven't tried to come that way."

"Well, then," Tim replied, "they'll just march down here when the Yankees show up."

"They may not have time," said Gramp. "If the Yankees move fast enough, they'll be in Richmond before our army can do anything about it."

But the Yankees didn't move fast. It took time to prepare the big army to march, and when it moved, it moved slowly. Parts of the Confederate army arrived in Yorktown in late March and began preparing to block the Yankees' advance.

Even so, each day Sally saw people from the

town passing by on the road with their wagons loaded with everything they could carry. "We're going to Richmond," some of them called. "You better get out too."

Mother sat everybody down at the dinner table. "Your Aunt Jane has invited us to come live in her house in Richmond. But Gramp and I have decided that we won't go until we have to," she said. "This house and farm are all we own. If we leave, the Yankees will burn everything that they can't steal."

Nora threw up her hands. "But Mama," she said, "if they march through while we're here, they'll do all that and kill us too."

"That's just talk, Nora," said Mama. "I can't believe they would kill women and children. But even so, I think we should prepare for the worst."

Mama brought out the most precious things they owned. "This silver tea set was a gift when your father and I were married. Here is the dress in which all three of you children were christened. My mother embroidered it. I think we should put them in a tin box and bury it in the garden. If we must leave, someday one of you can come back for it."

Mama opened a little box, showing them two rings and a locket. "These rings belonged to your grandmother. The locket has her picture inside." She handed one of the rings to Nora and the other to

Sally. "You girls should have them. Hide them if the Yankees come. I will wear the locket."

Sally had seen the rings before. Mother had given her the silver one and Nora the gold. Sally was glad, because she thought the silver was prettier. The band had a filigree decoration of little flowers set around a shiny violet stone.

"There's nothing for me," complained Tim.

"Well, here then," Gramp said. "You can have my old pocketknife." He winked. "The pirate Jean Lafitte gave it to me in the War of 1812. He was on our side. Wish he was alive today. He'd never have let the Yankees take New Orleans."

Tim stared at the knife as if it was made of gold. "But Gramp," he said, "you'll need this."

"What for?" Gramp said. "Haven't skinned a rabbit in years. All I do with it is whittle."

"I'll stab a Yankee with it, if they come," said Tim.

"You'll do nothing of the kind," Mama said. "If you see any Yankees, your job is to take the cows out of the barn and drive them as far away as you can. Along with yourself. Is that understood?"

"Yes, ma'am," he said meekly.

"Now you and Sally go out and dig a hole while I find a tin box to bury the other things."

As they were digging, a few bees flew lazily past

Sally. "Tim," she said, "I have an idea. Do you want to set a trap for the Yankees?"

"Sure do," he said.

She explained her plan, and Tim went off to find a coil of rope.

They were just in time. That night, as Sally was in bed, she could hear the boom of cannons as the Yankee army reached Yorktown. The war was headed right toward them.

In the morning, Mama started to pack. "We can't take much," she said. "Only what will fit in the wagon, and the lighter it is, the faster we can go."

Sally had no trouble packing, but Nora couldn't decide what to take. "If we're going to live in Richmond," she said, "I have to look my best. There will be dances to go to."

"You just need one party dress," Sally said.

"You don't understand," Nora told her. "I need petticoats and a hoop skirt. And it would be impossible to appear in public in just one dress. What would people think?"

Nora was still trying to fit all her things into a trunk when Sally heard loud shouts outside the house. "Oh-oh," she said. "I think you'd better make up your mind soon, Nora."

"Why?"

"The Yankees are here." Sally ran downstairs.

Gramp was at the front door, trying to hold it closed. But the four soldiers in blue uniforms forced their way past him.

They weren't as nice as Southern boys, Sally thought. It made her angry to see them looking around and picking up things as if they owned the house. One of them started to pull open the drawers in the sideboard. "Where's your gold and silver?" he said.

"We haven't got any," Mama replied stoutly. "We're only farmers."

"You're lying," the soldier said. "Where's your men?"

"Gone to fight the Yankees," Gramp said, and the soldiers laughed. Sally looked around. Tim wasn't there. She hoped he'd gone to move the cows.

"We're hungry," another soldier said. "Give us a ham."

"We haven't had any hams since last year," Mama told them. "Stop that!" she shouted to a soldier who was taking some of Papa's books off the shelves. The man laughed and threw them on the floor.

"What's upstairs?" asked another one.

Sally didn't want them to find Nora. She'd probably faint. "Mama, don't you have some apple pie?" Sally said.

"That's right," said Mama. "I'll give you some pie

and the leftover chicken. We don't have anything else."

"Bring it all out," said a soldier, and Mama left the room.

"You're all a pack of cowards," Gramp said. One of the men gave him a shove that sent him sprawling onto the sofa.

"Don't hurt him," Sally called. "I'll tell you where the silver and gold are."

They all looked at her. "It's buried in the garden," she said. "A big trunk full of it. Right next to the beehives. You'll see it. The shovel is still there."

"Sally!" said Gramp. "How could you tell them that?"

When the Yankees heard that, they smiled. "You'll find it," Sally told them eagerly. "It's more than you can carry."

One of the soldiers started for the door. The others glanced at each other. "You'd better not be lyin'," one of them warned, and then they all ran out to catch up with the other one, the pie and chicken forgotten.

As soon as they were gone, Sally said, "Push a chair or something against the door, Gramp. Keep them from getting back in."

"That won't stop them," he said. "Why did you–?"

"I'll tell you later," Sally said, and rushed back up the stairs to her bedroom.

Nora was hiding under the bed. Sally could see her shoes sticking out. "Sally?" Nora called. "What's happening? Have they gone?"

Sally ignored her and went to the window. Earlier, she and Tim had attached ropes to the beehives and strung them up here. Now she took hold of the ropes and watched as the Yankees came running through the garden. One of them took the shovel that she had left leaning against the hives. The others pointed to the fresh patch of earth where they had buried Mama's treasures.

Sally pulled hard on the ropes, praying that her plan would work. The ropes stretched tight, and Sally could see the hives move a little. She gathered up the ropes and jerked them as hard as she could.

The hives toppled over and crashed on the ground. At once, the angry bees flew out. As Sally hoped they would, the bees headed straight for the soldiers. The Yankees began to slap themselves and jump around, screaming. But by moving around, they only attracted more bees. Pretty soon, a whole cloud of them was stinging each soldier, and the Yankees began to run.

Sally started to laugh. She couldn't help herself. "Head for the river!" she called after them. She looked over at the barn, and there was Tim waving at her. He had watched the whole thing.

Sally turned around and told Nora to come out from under the bed. "We've got to leave right now," Sally said. "Before the Yankees come back."

Chapter 7
Farewell

Sally and Tim helped lug Nora's trunk down the stairs. "What have you got in here?" Tim complained. "A horse?"

"You wouldn't understand," Nora told him airily. "It's women's things. I may be invited to a dance."

"If you wear whatever's in here, you won't be able to walk, much less dance," he said. "All I have to take is my drum."

"If there's anything we should leave behind, that's it," muttered Nora.

Gramp helped them hoist the trunk onto the wagon. "I'm sorry I shouted at you when the Yankees were here," he said to Sally. "I didn't know what you were up to. Why didn't you tell us earlier?"

"We were afraid that you wouldn't want us to tip over the beehives," Sally said.

Gramp chuckled. "It won't hurt the bees. They'll

repair the damage and make honey long after we've gone. But I'm sorry about the cows. I guess some Yankees will make a meal out of them. And Jake. It might be kinder to shoot him than to leave him."

"Jake?" asked Sally. "Aren't we going to take him?"

"We can't. He's too old and slow to keep up. We'll have to set him free and hope he finds enough grass to eat."

"Can I tell him good-bye?" asked Sally.

"Don't be long. Your ma is bringing her pots and pans, and that's all this wagon will hold. We've got to hurry."

Sally got a carrot and went down to the barn and took Jake out of his stall. She led him outside and removed his bridle. He nuzzled her, and she fed him the carrot. "Oh, Jake," she said. "What's going to happen to you? I hope the Yankees won't find you. I hate this war."

She looked out over the fields, where the corn was starting to come up. Every day of her whole life she had seen those fields from her window in the morning. She knew how they changed in every season of the year. And now maybe she'd never see them again.

Sally began to cry, and Jake nudged her. He wanted to go for a ride. She turned and kissed him and then ran up the hill to where the others were waiting.

Traveling to Richmond was slower than they had thought it would be. Many other people were headed west along the road to escape the war. Some were walking with packs over their shoulders. Others, like the Bradfords, rode in wagons, but people had thrown away things to lighten the load.

Strewn along the side of the road were bed-boards, mattresses, mirrors, chairs, tables, and even an old sofa with its stuffing leaking out.

Sometimes there were abandoned wagons with broken wheels. Trunks stood open where people had left them. Dresses, shoes, and curtains were scattered in the muddy ditch. A doll that had fallen in the middle of the road was crushed flat by a wagon wheel.

At the same time, Confederate troops were marching the other way, to fight the Yankees. The Bradfords had to pull their wagon to the side to let them pass. "Go get the Yankees!" Tim called, and some of the soldiers gave him a salute. He looked after them longingly. Sally knew Tim wished he were marching with them.

When night fell, the Bradfords pulled their wagon into a field. Mama had brought some biscuits and honey and strawberries. "We should save some for the morning," she said. "We won't be able to get any other food before we reach Richmond."

Tim and Gramp spread their blankets on the ground. Sally went to sleep in the wagon with Nora and Mama. She was still hungry. All night she dreamed of Jake starving to death because she couldn't give him a carrot.

In the morning they ate the last of their food. Tim and Sally found some blackberries and shared them with the others. But it wasn't enough. As the sun rose in the sky, Sally's stomach began to rumble. "How long will it be till we get to Richmond?" she asked Mama.

"I hope we'll be there tonight," Mama said. The others were hungry too. In the afternoon, Gramp had to let Mama drive the wagon while he lay down in the back.

Night fell, but they went on. "If we stop," Mama said, "we'll just be hungrier tomorrow."

At last they saw some houses where lamps burned inside. They stopped and Tim knocked on one of the doors. When he came back, he told them that Richmond was only half a mile away. "I told them we were hungry," he said, "but they said that everybody coming to Richmond was hungry. They had no more food to give away."

Mama shook her head. "I'd never turned away anyone who came to my door wanting food."

Richmond wasn't like Yorktown. Sally had never seen such a big place before. There were rows and rows of houses and so many streets that she couldn't imagine how you would find your way around.

Most of the houses were dark. The only places that were open were taverns. Rough-looking men stood outside talking loudly.

Gramp was still asleep, and Sally was worried about him. "Mama," she asked, "where is Aunt Jane's house?"

"It's on Spring Street," Mama said. "I was there before, but I don't know the way."

"Stop the wagon," Sally said. "Tim, go over and ask one of those men where Spring Street is."

Tim looked at her. Sally could see he was as afraid as she was. "I'll go with you," she said.

"Sally!" Mama warned her, but Sally had already jumped down. Tim hurried to catch up.

"I'll do the talking," Tim whispered. They approached a group of three men. Sally could smell whiskey on their breaths.

"Sir, could you tell us how to find Spring Street?" asked Tim.

"Lost, eh?" one of the men said. "Where you from?"

"We came up from Yorktown," Tim said.

"What you got in that wagon?"

"Just our clothes and Gramp's favorite chair," Tim said.

"How about money?"

"We haven't got any."

"Costs money to live here, boy. Everything has a high price. How 'bout you gimme a dollar to tell you where Spring Street is?" The other men laughed.

Sally was angry. "We thought we'd find Southern gentlemen in Richmond," she said. Tim nudged her with his elbow.

But one of the other men stepped forward. "He's just joking with you," he said. "Go on down here for three more streets and turn right. Spring's the second street off to the left."

"Thank you," said Sally. The man touched the brim of his hat. "Good thing you left Yorktown," he said. "Yankees took it yesterday."

With Tim and Sally pointing out the way, Mama

found Aunt Jane's house. It was dark too, but when they knocked for a few minutes, a flickering lamp appeared at the window. "Who's there?" a voice called.

"It's Mary," Mama said. "I'm here with the children."

Sally heard the bolt slide open. There stood a short, round-faced woman in her nightdress. "Oh my," she said. "I wish I'd known you'd be here tonight."

"We had to leave in a hurry," Mama said. "Will's father is in the wagon. I think he's ill. We haven't had anything to eat since this morning."

"Bring him in," Aunt Jane said. "Quickly. The streets can be dangerous at night. Take the wagon down the alley and put the horses into the stable."

Sally and Tim put the wagon away and came through the back door to the kitchen. A plate of sandwiches sat on the table. Sally had to keep herself from grabbing one.

"This is all I have in the house," said Aunt Jane. "But it'll put something in your stomachs."

When she passed the plate, Sally took a sandwich and bit into it. It wasn't what she expected. Tim grunted as he tasted his.

Aunt Jane smiled. "They're cold sliced turnip sandwiches, I'm afraid. Tomorrow we'll go out and try to find something else. It's hard to find any kind of food in Richmond, but I have a friend."

Sally thought of the chickens and cows and corn on their farm. The Yankees would be eating them by now. She hated this war.

Chapter 8
Richmond

Mama was shocked to learn that Aunt Jane had a job. "There was no other way to make ends meet, dear sister," Aunt Jane said. "When Amos died, he left me this house and a little money. But everything in Richmond has become so expensive since the war. Besides, the work I do is writing letters in a government office. I think of it as my part in the war."

Tim spoke up. "I can get a job too, Mama," he said. "We need the money."

Mama thought about it. "I guess we all have to adjust. I hadn't thought about what it would mean to leave the farm."

"Today is Saturday," said Aunt Jane. "Nora and Sally can go to the market with me. Mary, you stay here and watch over Gramp. Give him some turnip broth, and by noon we'll be back with something better to eat."

Sally and Nora put on their bonnets and went out with Aunt Jane. In the daylight, the streets of Richmond were crowded with people. It almost seemed as if more of them were selling things than buying. Women spread rugs, tablecloths, and clothing in front of their houses. A man with a barrel was ladling out sacks of something to a line of people. "Flour," said Aunt Jane. "But it is probably full of weevils."

She led them down a side street to a shop with no name outside. A sign on the window read, "Closed," but Aunt Jane pulled a string beside the door and Sally heard a bell ring inside.

A face peeked out from behind the shade that covered the window. Then the door opened and Aunt Jane led them inside. It was dark here, but Sally saw a thin, bent-over man wearing black pants held up by suspenders. He had no coat, and the sleeves of his white shirt were turned up and held with garters.

"This is Mr. Franz, girls," Aunt Jane said. "Max, these are my nieces. They've just arrived with my sister and her family."

Mr. Franz spoke with a thick German accent. "Ach, everyone in Richmond has visitors. Too many people. Too little food. The Yankees burn all our farms, and the blockade…." He shrugged.

"The *Virginia* is going to break the blockade,"

said Sally. "We saw it."

"No, no," Mr. Franz said. "The *Virginia,* she's at the bottom of the bay. No good now."

"What? How could any ship sink the *Virginia?*" asked Sally.

"The Confederates did it themselves," Mr. Franz said. "When they saw the Yankees marching into Norfolk, they drilled holes in the bottom. See, it was better to sink it than to let the Yankees have it." He shook his head. "The blockade will only get worse now."

"But, Max, you'll still be able to get flour and sugar and meat and tea, won't you?" Aunt Jane asked.

He spread his hands. "One can always obtain such things... for a price. There are blockade runners who unload their ships on the shore at night. Or when a Yankee official inspects the cargo, sometimes he will look the other way–for a price." Mr. Franz shook his finger at Sally. "Sadly, there are people who use the war to make money for themselves."

"We don't have any money," Sally said. "We had to leave our farm ... everything."

"Don't worry," Aunt Jane said. "Max will help us. Won't you?"

Mr. Franz nodded slowly. "If I can," he said. He looked at Sally and Nora. "Your aunt's husband, may his soul rest in peace, lent me money years ago to start my business. I had just come here from Germany, and like you now, I had to leave in a hurry. He was the only one who would help me. So, let us see."

He took out a notebook and leafed through it. "I can give you a small ham, one chicken, half a pound of flour, a little sugar. Maybe I can find some butter and eggs, if you don't tell anyone."

Sally's mouth watered.

After Mr. Franz had wrapped the food, Aunt Jane opened her purse and placed some money on the counter. "I only have thirty-five dollars, Max," she said. "I know it's not enough."

"Not enough!" Nora exclaimed. "Why, in Yorktown that would buy a month's worth of food."

Aunt Sally shook her head. "Not in Richmond, dear," she said. "And we're lucky that Max will let me owe him the rest."

"How are we ever going to live here?" Nora wailed.

Aunt Sally paid her no attention. "Max, I have a nephew too. He's a big strong boy and says he's willing to work."

"We'll see, we'll see," said Mr. Franz. "Can he handle horses?"

"Oh yes," Sally said.

"I'll ask a man I know with a stable," Mr. Franz said. He took off his glasses and polished them. Putting them back on, he peered closely at Nora. She took a step backward.

"Excuse me, miss," he said. "I know this may seem strange to you. I do not mean to be rude. You have lovely hair."

Nora put both hands to her hair and blushed. Sally thought she shouldn't act so surprised. Everybody said Nora had beautiful hair. It was thick, and long, and the color of cornsilk. Sally had always envied her.

"I mention that," Mr. Franz went on, "only because there are people in Richmond who make wigs. You understand, they would pay for your hair."

"For my hair?" Nora said. "You mean to cut it off?"

"Not all of it," said Mr. Franz. "And of course, it grows back." He rubbed his own head, which had only a few white strands of hair, and smiled. "For you, it will grow back."

"I ... I ... I," stammered Nora.

"She'll think about it," said Aunt Jane, nudging Nora toward the door. "Thank you again, Max, for everything."

"Good deeds are rewarded," he said.

During the next few days, they settled in at Aunt Jane's. Gramp felt better after a couple of good meals, and began going to the Confederate Congress each day to hear the latest news. Tim started work at the stables and was proud to bring home his wages. Sally wanted to work too, so Aunt Jane found some cloth and let her begin making bandages for the soldiers' hospital in Richmond.

Mama was very worried that Papa and Rob would not know where they had gone. She wrote them letters, but there was no telling when they would receive them.

For a while, it looked as if Richmond itself would not be safe. The Yankee army kept moving up the peninsula, and by the end of May it was only a few miles from Richmond. At night the campfires of the Yankee soldiers could be seen as a glow in the sky. For the first time, Sally wondered if the South might lose the war.

Then one day Gramp came home from the Congress with news. "They've finally stopped all their arguments and done the smart thing," he said. "They put Robert Lee in charge of the army. Should've done that long ago."

He was right. Within a month, Lee rallied the Confederate forces and boldly attacked the Yankees. For the first time since Sally had been in Richmond, people seemed cheerful. When news came that the Yankees were retreating, Confederate flags waved from the front porches of houses. That Sunday in church, the minister led them in a prayer of thanksgiving for the victory.

Finally, in August, they got a letter from Papa. "Glad to hear you are safe in Richmond," Mama read aloud. "As for our farm, we can only trust in God. The Yankees can burn and steal, but they cannot take the land away. Someday this war will be over and we can start anew." Mama put down the letter and wiped her eyes.

"Where are they?" Tim asked.

"He doesn't say," said Mama. She picked up the letter and read it to herself. "He says Rob was sick," she told them. "The food was bad, and many of the men were ill."

Mama read the last lines aloud. "But we are all fine now. Everyone is ready to follow Lee. I cannot write more, but we will soon be moving north, I believe. Our love to all of you."

"Moving north!" Gramp exclaimed. "That's the ticket. If Lee can bring the war into Yankee territory, Lincoln will have to give up."

That was Lee's plan. In August he led his troops across the Potomac River into Maryland. For the first time, a Southern army had invaded a Northern state.

But then the news stopped coming. Nobody seemed to know where Lee was going next. Rumors spread through Richmond. Some said that Lee was heading down the Potomac into Washington. Others said he was marching farther north into Pennsylvania.

It was a month before anyone learned what had happened. Every day Gramp would go down to the telegraph office to wait with the crowd outside. Finally he came home with bad news. "Lee met the Northern army at Sharpsburg, near Antietam Creek in Maryland. It was a big battle. Lots of men killed.

Thousands. Tens of thousands, maybe."

Gramp sat down in the chair that they had brought from the front porch of their house. Sally thought that he looked as if he would never get up again. "I think we lost," he said.

The battle at Antietam was the worst day of the whole war. More than 12,000 soldiers in Lee's army had been killed or wounded. It took a week before all their names were posted at the telegraph office. Gramp wouldn't go, so Sally and Nora went down to read through the long lists, looking for the names of someone they loved.

One afternoon Sally heard Nora scream and turn away from the window of the telegraph office. Sally looked at the list. It read: "WILKINS, JACK, of Yorktown." Nora's boyfriend. He had been killed.

Nora cried all night. No one could comfort her. In the morning Sally said, "We've got to go to the telegraph office, Nora. Rob's name might be on the list. Or…." She couldn't say Papa's name.

"You go," said Nora. "I can't bear it."

So Sally went alone. She pressed toward the front of the crowd every time another long sheet of yellow paper was posted in the window. All day she scanned the lists, name after name after name, fearing that the next one would be "BRADFORD." But as the sun set, she ran home with the news that Papa and Rob were safe. So far.

When Sally returned to Aunt Jane's house, Nora wasn't there. She had gone out earlier without telling anyone. "She's so upset," said Mama. "I don't know what she might do."

They found out soon enough. Nora came home and put some money on Mama's lap. Then she took off her hat. Her long beautiful hair was gone, cut so short that she couldn't even pin it up.

"Oh, Nora," Mama said.

"It's all right, Mama," said Nora. "And I have something else to tell you. I went to the hospital. They need women to tend the wounded. I found a job."

Chapter 9
The Bread Riot

Spring came again, 1863. Sally missed turning over the garden and seeing the forsythias bloom beside the front porch. They had lived in Aunt Jane's house for a year, and the war was still going on. At least Papa and Rob were still alive. Letters came from them about once a month.

After Nora had been working in the hospital for a few weeks, Mama started going there too. "I can't be idle when everybody else is doing something," she said. "Will and Rob are fighting. This is my duty."

She was needed, for almost every day lines of wagons came into Richmond with the wounded and sick soldiers. Late at night, when they thought Sally was asleep, Mama and Nora talked quietly about the horrible things they saw at the hospital.

Tim had grown tall in the past year. Though he was still earning money at the stable, he was unhappy. The other day, a girl taunted him when he unhitched her horses from her wagon. "What's the matter with you?" she said.

He didn't understand what she meant at first. Then she said, "My brother was killed at Sharpsburg. At least he wasn't a coward. Where are you going to hide if the Yankees take Richmond?"

Tim told Sally the story that night. "She was right," he said. "I'm nearly 15. I'm full grown. I've made up my mind to join the army."

"No, Tim," Sally said. "You can't. Mama would never let you. You're too young."

"There's lots as young as me in the army by now," he said. "Lee needs every man he can get. People say he's going to go north again this year."

"What good will it do?" said Sally. "The Yankees beat him before. They have more soldiers than the South does."

"That's why I have to go," he said. "If we lost, people will always point me out as a coward. Promise me you won't tell Mama."

Reluctantly, Sally gave her word. And a few days later, Tim didn't come home from work. Later that evening, one of his friends brought them a note.

It was short. "I'm going to join Papa and Rob," it read. "Don't worry about me, Mama. I'll be careful."

Mama was frantic. "Sally, get the horses out,"

Mama said. "We'll go after Tim in the wagon."

"Mama, we don't know which way to look," said Nora. "If he's determined to do this, you can't stop him."

Gramp sat up in his chair. "Be proud of him, Mary," he said.

"Proud?" Mama said. "You men and your war. You don't know what those boys look like down at the hospital, with arms or legs torn off. Broken apart like toys. What if Tim comes home like that? It was hard enough to see Will and Rob leave, but Tim is a boy."

"There aren't any boys on the battlefield," Gramp said. "I wish he'd said good-bye, though."

Sally felt lonely after Tim left. Mama and Nora spent all day at the hospital. Gramp sat in his chair dozing and reading the newspaper. Sally kept making bandages, but it was boring work.

Twice a week she went to Mr. Franz's store with Aunt Sally. He had less and less to give them. "It's the blockade," he said. "Flour and sugar are worth more than gold now."

One day Sally woke up to hear angry shouts in the street outside. She rushed to the window. A crowd of women were marching down the street, waving sticks and axes. "Our children are starving," she heard one of them yell. "We want bread!"

Sally dressed quickly and went outside, running after the crowd. The women had swarmed into the market square and were throwing stones through store windows. When a shopkeeper came outside, the crowd knocked him to the ground. Some women went inside his store and began carrying food out.

The crowd cheered. "Take the food!" somebody shouted. "They're all robbers anyway. They're getting rich by making us starve!"

In a few minutes there was broken glass all over the square. More people joined the mob, and soon women were running every which way carrying sacks of flour, baskets of fruit, cheeses, ducks and chickens–anything they could get their hands on.

Sally ran toward the little street where Mr. Franz's store was. The mob hadn't reached it yet. She pulled the doorbell string and Mr. Franz unlocked the door. "Something terrible is happening," she told him. "There's a mob of women in the market square breaking into stores."

He stepped outside. They could hear the shouts and the sound of breaking glass in the next block. "Come in," Mr. Franz said. "Quick."

He led her into the back room and pointed to a stack of boards. "Bring them out," he said. "I'll get a hammer." She helped him nail the boards over the inside of the windows. He started to put a board over the door. "Do you want to stay?" he asked Sally.

She thought for a second. "No. Mama will worry about me."

"All right," he said. "Take this." He gave her a ham. "Tell your aunt not to come here until it's safe. And…I thank you."

Sally smiled and slipped out the door. She ran up the street with the ham. At the corner, she stopped to look around.

Soldiers with rifles were marching down the main street toward the crowd. At first, the women started to draw back. Then one of them stepped out in front and shouted at the soldiers. "Are you going to shoot us?" she screamed. "Is that what you're here for? Go ahead. Tell your mothers that you shot at hungry women. Tell them you were afraid to fight the Yankees!" She took a stone from the ground and threw it at them.

Sally saw the soldiers hesitate and then lower their guns. A cheer went up from the crowd, and the women headed for the next row of stores.

Before they reached it, however, a carriage drawn by two black horses appeared at the far end of the street. The driver headed straight for the angry mob. Sally hurried to get out of its way.

The carriage came to a halt, and a thin man with a wispy beard stepped out. Murmurs spread through the crowd. "The president. It's the president."

Sally recognized him, for his picture hung in many of the stores of Richmond. It was Jefferson Davis, president of the Confederacy.

The women pressed forward, shouting angrily, and surrounded him. An officer led several soldiers through the crowd, pushing people aside. With their help, Davis climbed onto the top of his carriage.

"This is disgraceful!" he shouted. "Go home, all of you!"

The crowd booed him. "We need to feed our children," someone shouted. "We can't afford to buy food! People are getting rich from our suffering."

"No one is getting rich!" Davis shouted back. "You say you are hungry and have no money—here is all I have." He reached in his pockets and threw coins and bills at the crowd. "That's all I have. Take it."

A few people scrambled for the money, but others shook their fists at the president. Sternly, he took his watch from his vest pocket. Sally thought he was going to throw that at them as well. Instead, he said, "This lawlessness must stop. I will give you five minutes to disperse. Then I will order the soldiers to fire."

Sally moved away. Although she hadn't stolen the ham, she was embarrassed to be carrying it.

Some of the women at the edges of the crowd began to leave. Davis motioned the soldiers forward.

They began to push the leaders of the crowd back. A few protested loudly, but when they saw others leaving, they gradually gave way.

Sally ran home as fast as she could. She told Aunt Jane what had happened. "I don't know what we'll do if Max closes his store," Aunt Jane said.

That evening, Sally sat down with her mother. "Mama, when you went to work at the hospital, you said it was your duty. Tim went to join the army because it was *his* duty. I feel ashamed because I'm the only one who's not doing anything to help."

"Why, you help Aunt Jane keep house," Mama said. "You bring Gramp his newspaper every day."

"That's not enough. I'm not a baby anymore, Mama. I want to work in the hospital too."

"Oh, Sally, you have no idea what it's like. It's not proper for a girl to be there."

"Nora does it."

"Well, she's older than you."

"Not that much older. Mama, I must do something. I must."

Mama put her arms around her. "Oh, this war has done such terrible things to my family," Mama said. "I don't know what to tell you."

"Let me try, Mama. If it's too hard, I'll stay home."

Mama sighed. "If you wish."

Chapter 10

The Hospital

Sally, Nora, and Mama took a horsecar to the hospital, a huge new red-brick building at the edge of town. When Sally saw it, she remembered what Mama had said about men torn apart like toys. She almost stopped when she and Mama and Nora reached the big wooden door, but she forced herself to go in. She told herself that she could close her eyes if she had to.

Inside, it was not as bad as she feared. As they walked down the hallway, she smelled alcohol and something else—maybe it was the ether that Mama said the doctors used to make people sleep.

Sally peeked inside one of the big rooms as a nurse came out the door. There were rows of beds, but a lot of them were empty.

Mama introduced her to the head nurse, Mrs. Pember. She was a tall woman with gray eyes that seemed very sad. "You're starting at a good time," Mrs. Pember told her. "There hasn't been a big battle since Sharpsburg. Most of our work now is tending soldiers who are ill or recovering from their wounds."

Mrs. Pember took Sally to the kitchen. "We'll start you off bringing water and food to the patients. Smile and give them a few words of encouragement. That's the best medicine we can give them, I'm afraid. We're very short of supplies, thanks to the blockade."

The food was only vegetable broth and rice, but nobody minded. Some of the men were so weak that Sally had to help feed them. Others wanted her to stop and talk.

"You look like my sister," one of the men said. He held up his hands, which were covered with bandages. "Could you bring some paper and help me write a letter?"

"I will when I'm finished serving the food," she said.

It took her so long that she nearly forgot about him. Patients kept asking Sally questions. Had she heard any news about Lee's army? She told them that Lee had gone north again, into Pennsylvania. Did the people in Richmond still support the war? Sally bit her tongue and told them that everyone knew the South would win.

When the meals were all served, Sally got some paper and ink from Mrs. Pember's office. She returned to the man who had asked her to write a letter. He gave her a name and address in South Carolina.

"Dear Mama and Sissy," he began. "Do not worry about me. I have been wounded but am now in the hospital in Richmond. My hands are hurt, so a pretty girl is writing this for me." He smiled at Sally, and went on.

"I was lucky because I saw a lot of men die and somehow I was spared. The doctors say that when my hands are healed I can come home. You are always in my thoughts."

The man looked down at the bandages on the ends of his arms. "You better stop there," he told Sally. "Sign it Love, Fred."

"I could write a longer letter," Sally said. "I know we always like to get letters from Papa and my brother."

He shook his head. "That's all. Better they don't know the truth."

Sally was puzzled. "What is the truth?"

The man lifted his arms. "The doctors cut off both my hands. They said they had to do it to save me. Save me for what?"

The man began to cry. "Go away now," he told

Sally. "Just make sure you send that letter."

She carried it inside the pocket of her dress until it was time to go home. After dinner, Sally got a stamp from Aunt Jane and took the letter to the post office.

The next day, Sally went back to tell the man she had mailed the letter. But his bed was empty. "Where did he go?" Sally asked the man in the bed next to his.

"Fred? He got sick with fever in the night, and they took him to another ward. Blood poisoning, I heard the doctor say. They cut off his hands to try to save him, but it spread."

After Sally finished her food deliveries that morning, she went to Mrs. Pember. "Where are the patients that have fever and blood poisoning?" Sally asked.

"You can't do anything for them," Mrs. Pember said. "They are too ill to eat. We need quinine to treat them, but we have none. All we can do is give them water. If they're very strong, they will live. But most won't."

"I have to tell this man that I sent his letter," Sally said.

"If he has fever, he won't be able to understand you," Mrs. Pember said. "Sally, I want to warn you about something. There's going to be a battle in

Pennsylvania soon. Afterward, many wounded men will be brought to the hospital. You haven't seen anything like this before. It will be horrifying."

"My brother and my father are probably going to be in that battle," Sally said. "Maybe both of my brothers. I don't care how horrible it is. I have to help in whatever way I can."

Mrs. Pember nodded. "They'd be proud of you," she said. "But if you feel that it's too much for you to bear, no one will blame you if you leave."

The name of the battle was Gettysburg. Gramp told them about it a few days later at dinnertime. "Lee almost won," he said. And from that, Sally knew that Lee had lost.

The next day, Sally was put to work making bandages and preparing fresh beds. Lee's army was retreating back into Virginia. Any day now, the wagonloads of sick and wounded men would arrive. Sally told herself that no matter how bad they looked, she wouldn't quit working.

The day it began was the longest in Sally's life. Carrying bandages to the operating room, she saw soldiers who had been brought inside and left lying on the floors. Their wounds had been bandaged with rags that were now dirty and soaking with blood. Some of the men cried out as she passed by. "I need water. Please. Give me something to drink." She heard others praying and crying.

Doctors went down the corridors, pointing at each man, telling how he was to be treated. Nurses carried some of them away to wash their wounds and give them fresh bandages. Others were taken to the operating room. Sally knew that meant their wounds were so bad that the surgeons would have to cut off an arm or leg.

A nurse came out of the operating room and handed Sally a pile of bloody uniforms. "Take these," she said, and went back inside. As the door closed, Sally heard a man screaming in pain.

Sally had already been told to put all the dirty clothes in a pile outside, where they would be burned. There, she saw soldiers lifting more men from a wagon. They left one behind.

"Wait!" Sally called. "Here's someone else!"

A soldier looked over his shoulder and told her, "He's dead."

Sally looked at the man. He seemed like a boy, really. Not much older than Tim. She had never seen a dead person before. His eyes were still half-open, and she remembered you were supposed to close them. She put her hand out and touched his face. It was still warm. She pressed his eyelids down and began to cry.

"I won't quit," she said to herself. "I won't!" She ran back inside.

It got worse as the day went on. Sally lost all track of time. No one in the hospital stopped to eat or rest. After a while, Sally learned to be careful running through the corridors, because the floors were slick with blood. She had stopped listening to the screams.

Sometime late in the afternoon, she took another load of bloody clothing to the yard in the back of the hospital. No one had time to burn it, and the pile of uniforms looked like a haystack. Strewn across the cobblestones were things that soldiers had carried in their pockets–Bibles, wallets, letters, tintype pictures of people.

Sally picked up one of the tintypes. It showed a young woman and a small boy. They were probably the wife and son of one of the soldiers. Every one of these objects meant that a soldier had someone he loved and wanted to remember.

And then she saw something, halfway up the pile of clothing, that made her heart stop. It was a red and blue sash, dirty and torn now, but Sally recognized it. She pulled it down.

It was Rob's sash. The one she had made him when he went off to war. There were his initials, R. B., that she had sewn.

Rob was here.

Sally ran back inside the hospital with the sash in her hands. She wanted to tell Mama, but she was in one of the operating rooms.

Sally was frantic. She ran down the corridors where the wounded men lay, looking for Rob. When she didn't find him, she tried to think. Rob must have been brought in earlier in the day, because the sash was halfway up the pile of clothing.

He could have been operated on, or he might be one of the men who weren't badly hurt. Then he would be in one of the rooms for new patients.

She rushed to that part of the hospital and started to search for him. Down the rows of beds in each room, she looked for Rob's face. She paid no attention when men called out to her, asking for water.

She almost missed him. Rob didn't look the way he had two years ago. She glanced at him and started to move to the next bed. But then she stopped and went closer. His face was thin and covered with red spots. His eyes were closed, and Sally shivered as she remembered the dead man in the wagon.

But Rob was alive. She saw him breathing. "Rob," she called. "Rob. It's me, Sally."

She couldn't wake him. Sally looked around and saw a nurse. She pulled her over to Rob's bed. "What's wrong with him?"

"Feel his forehead," the nurse instructed.

"It's hot," Sally told her.

"He has typhus," the nurse said. "We can't do anything but let him rest. In a week, he might get better." The nurse shrugged. "Or he may not."

"You mean he'll die?" Sally asked.

The nurse nodded.

"Can't you give him any medicine?"

"There's only one thing that might help, and we don't have it here," the nurse told her.

"What's that?"

"Quinine."

"Where can you get it?"

"Nowhere. I told you. We had some earlier, but the Yankee blockade cut off our supplies. That's the only thing that will cure typhus. Just let him rest."

Sally stayed behind as the nurse walked away. She took Rob's hand. It felt hot too. "Rob?" she said. "Can you hear me?"

She thought she felt his hand squeeze hers a little.

"I'm going to get you some quinine, Rob," Sally said. "I don't know how, but I'm going to do it."

Chapter 11

On the River

There was no time to lose. Sally remembered that Mrs. Pember had told her she could leave if she had to. She couldn't stop to find Mama or Nora.

She got her bonnet and took the horsecar back into town. There was one person who might have some quinine—Mr. Franz.

His shop was still closed, but Sally rang the bell, hoping he was there. Sure enough, he peeped out the window and opened the door.

His smile vanished from his face as he looked at her. "Sally! What happened? Are you hurt?"

She looked down and saw that her dress had blood on it. "No, no," she explained. "I've been working in the hospital. My brother Rob is there."

"He was in the battle, then? The casualty lists are terrible. People are saying that tens of thousands of men were killed. Is he…?"

Sally shook her head. "He's alive, but unconscious. He wasn't wounded, but he has something that the nurse called typhus."

Mr. Franz nodded grimly. "Typhus. Yes, it comes when people have to drink dirty water. It's a terrible thing. What can I do to help?"

"The nurse says Rob should have quinine, but there isn't any at the hospital. I thought that maybe–" Her heart sank as she saw him shake his head.

"All the medicine I had is gone," he said. "If I myself were sick, I would have none to take."

"Do you know anybody in Richmond who might have some?"

"The doctors have already sent their supplies to the hospital." Mr. Franz put his hand to his forehead. "Please. Come inside. I have thought of something."

He put on his glasses and went to a small desk in the corner of the room. Sally followed and saw him open a ledger that looked like an account book. Each page had a name and address and columns of figures.

Mr. Franz turned the pages slowly until he found the one he was looking for. He carefully copied the name and address down on a small piece of paper and handed it to Sally. "This is a place where you can find a person who would have quinine. Ask them for the Earl. They'll know how to find him."

"Earl? What's his last name?" Sally asked.

"No, no. The Earl. He's English, the son of a nobleman."

She looked at the address. "I don't know where this street is."

"It's not in Richmond. It is in Norfolk."

"Norfolk!" She stared at him. "But the Yankees have occupied Norfolk."

Mr. Franz nodded. "Yes. This man is a blockade runner, a smuggler, and who knows what else. He bribes the Yankee officials when he has to. But if you need something very badly, he is the person who will have it. Quinine, yes, certainly. Perhaps your other brother...Tim is his name? He could go there, to Norfolk."

"He's gone off to join the army too."

"Ah. Then your grandfather, or someone you trust. He could take a boat down the river."

Sally nodded. Gramp would not be strong enough. She had an idea, but it was so daring that she tried not to think about it too much. There were too many reasons why she shouldn't do it.

"Going down the river would be easy enough," Sally said. "But how would this person get back?"

"It is safe along the river right now. The Yankees patrol the banks in their part of it. If this person had a horse, the trip might take only three days."

Three days! But Rob's life depended on it. Sally

started toward the door.

Mr. Franz stopped her. "I must tell you one other thing," he said. "The Earl doesn't care who wins the war. He wants only to make money. He will ask for gold, not Confederate paper money."

"How much?" asked Sally.

"Five dollars, I think, would be enough." When he saw Sally's look of dismay, Mr. Franz took a key from his vest pocket. He unlocked a small metal box and took out a coin. "Here," he said. "I will add it to your aunt's bill."

It was a five-dollar Yankee gold piece. "Thank you," she said. "I'll pay it back. I promise."

He smiled. "When you can. Go now and tell your grandfather."

She hurried to Aunt Jane's house. Gramp was asleep in his chair, and Aunt Jane was at her job. It would be better not to wake Gramp, Sally thought. But then Mama would be frantic.

She smiled to herself. Mama will be frantic anyway. But they should all know that Rob was in the hospital.

She changed into some of Tim's clothes and tucked her hair under a cap. After she filled her pockets with apples and pecans, she shook Gramp's shoulder. He woke slowly, blinking at her.

"Tim?" he said. "You've come back?"

"No, it's Sally, Gramp. I want you to remember to tell Mama something."

He peered at her strangely. "Why are you dressed that way?"

"I have to go someplace. I'll be all right. I want you to tell Mama that Rob is in the hospital, and I have gone to get him medicine."

"Rob?" Gramp looked more and more confused. "In the hospital?"

"Yes. Mama will tell you all about it later. Remember, I've gone away to get him medicine. I'll be back in two or three days."

"Medicine," he repeated. "Yes, I'll remember."

She kissed him on the cheek. "Don't worry about me," she said.

"You'll need some money," Gramp said. "If you're going to be gone long."

"I have some," she said.

But he pressed some paper money into her hand. "I don't need this," he said. "You never can tell. Everything costs money nowadays."

He was right. She spent nearly half the money he gave her at the wharf by the river. Two boys who had been fishing were tying up their rowboat. She asked them if they would let her borrow it.

They laughed. "You think we're stupid? What if you steal it?" She was annoyed that they were so rude, and then she realized that they thought she was a boy. That was good, at least.

"I'll pay you," she said.

They glanced at each other. "How much?" one of them asked.

Gramp had given her twenty-five dollars. That had been a lot of money before the war, but now a bag of sugar cost ten dollars. "I'll give you ten dollars to let me use it till tomorrow," she said.

"Lemme see it," the bigger boy said.

She was careful not to let him see how much she had in her pocket and held out two five-dollar bills. He snatched them out of her hand.

She climbed down into the boat and the two boys pushed it away from the wharf. When she took the oars and began to row, the boys shouted, "We would've sold it to you for that! Dumb!"

She smiled and waved, as if she didn't mind that they were laughing at her. The joke would be on them.

Rob had taught her to row on the little river near their farm. It wasn't hard here, because she was going downstream. All she had to do was keep the boat from going aground. But she soon found that it leaked, and every so often she had to use a rusty bait bucket to bail it out.

Now that she had started, all the reasons why she shouldn't be doing this came rushing into her head.

She shivered when she thought what Mama would say.

Sally ate an apple to help herself feel better. She didn't know when she could get more food, so she chewed it down to the core. Her stomach growled, wanting more.

Near Richmond, the river wound back and forth like a snake. She knew that farther down it became straighter and wider. She hoped to get to that part before dark so it would be easier to steer. The farther she went tonight, the sooner she would get to Norfolk tomorrow.

Night fell just about the time she saw the lights of another town. That was Hopewell. Below here, the river would be wider. The moon rose in the sky, and she was glad to see that it was nearly full. By now there were no other boats on the river. She rowed to the middle, pulled up the oars and let the boat drift in the current.

She lay back and looked at the stars. Somewhere, she thought, maybe Tim would be looking up at them too. She tried to remember the last time everybody in her family had been together. Before the war. A long time ago. She fell asleep and the river carried her on.

Chapter 12

The Blockade Runner

Sally awoke when the rain started. It was morning, but the sky was gray and she had no idea what time it was. Her boat had run aground on a sandbar, which was lucky because the bottom was full of water.

She ate another apple and a handful of pecans and began to bail out the boat. The rain fell harder, and it seemed as if it was filling up the boat faster than she could bail.

This was a crazy idea, she thought. What if she did get to Norfolk and couldn't find the Earl? What if he was off somewhere, running the blockade? What if he had no quinine? What if…?

She forced herself to stop thinking that way. No more "what ifs." That was something Mama had once told her. "There's a lot of reasons not to do something that's hard," Mama had said. "But if it's worth doing, then you won't let the what ifs get in your way."

And saving Rob's life—that was worth doing.

Feeling better, she pushed the boat off the sand-bar. At least there was no problem finding her way. Just follow the river till she reached Hampton Roads. Norfolk was just south of there.

The rain kept getting heavier. It took all her energy to keep bailing the boat. She was worried. This looked like one of those terrible storms that sometimes came up the coast from the Caribbean. It seemed like the current was moving faster too.

What if she couldn't land the boat at Norfolk and was swept out to sea? "Stop it!" she shouted angrily at herself. "Just stop."

Sally was frightened for a minute when she could no longer see either bank of the river. But then she realized that meant she had reached the bay. Norfolk was down to her left. All she had to do was row.

There were waves here, and her boat bobbed up and down. But she had gotten stronger in the last two years, having to do so much of the farm work. This wasn't any harder than a day hoeing the cornfield, she thought to herself.

Then she heard a shout that seemed to come from right above her head. She looked up and saw a big ship bearing down on her out of the storm. She pulled in her oar on that side just in time to keep it from being snapped off. Two sailors looked over the rail of the ship, cursing at her.

Fortunately, the wake of the ship pushed her in the direction she wanted to go. She could see the docks now. That must be Norfolk.

As she drew closer to the shore, the water became a little calmer. She pulled on the oars with all her strength, looking over her shoulder to guide herself to the docks. Closer, closer now. Almost there. One more pull.

And she was in between the pilings. She had made it. She guided the boat toward a ladder and caught hold of it. She nearly slipped and fell as she stood up, but she used the ladder to keep her balance. It wouldn't matter if I did fall in, she thought. I'm soaked through to the skin anyway. She clambered up the ladder, leaving the boat behind.

"Hey!" someone on the dock shouted at her. It was a man in a slicker, a rubber coat that reached to his ankles. She wished she had one of those.

"You've lost your boat!" the man said.

"It doesn't matter," Sally said. "I have to find someone. Can you tell me where this address is?" She reached into her pocket, but when she pulled out the sheet of paper Mr. Franz had given her, it was as soaked as her clothes.

Carefully, Sally unfolded it, but the ink had run, making the address almost impossible to read. The man looked at it and shook his head. "Can you remember what it was?"

She tried to think. "Forty-four," she said. "Forty-four…something street."

The man took the ragged paper and peered at it. "Looks like…maybe it said 'River.' Was that it? Forty-four River Street?"

"I think so," said Sally. She hoped so.

"Well, that's not far," the man said. "That's River Street at the end of the dock. Forty-four would be down past the next cross street. Second building from the corner."

"Thank you," Sally said.

"You better get inside," the man told her. "There's a bad storm blowing up."

A bad storm? "This is already bad enough for me," Sally said.

"Oh, it'll get lots worse," he told her cheerfully.

There was no number over the door at Forty-four River Street. But it was open, so Sally went inside, glad at least to get out of the rain.

She nearly turned and went right back out. It was a tavern, with rough-looking seamen sitting at tables. The air was thick with smoke from their pipes. Several of the men looked in her direction. "Look what the storm blew into port," someone said, and the others laughed.

A woman carrying a tray came over to Sally and said, "Out of here, sonny. No begging allowed. Don't bother my customers."

"I'm not a beggar," Sally said indignantly.

"Hear that?" one of the men said. "He's not a beggar." That brought another laugh.

Sally lowered her voice. "I'm looking for the Earl." It sounded strange when she said it, but the woman's face changed. She looked closer at Sally and then reached out and tucked a strand of hair back under Tim's cap. "Come with me," she said.

They went into a back room, and the woman shut the door. "What's a girl like you want with the Earl?"

"I need to buy medicine for my brother," Sally said. "He'll die without it."

The woman frowned. "The Earl won't care about your brother. He'll want money."

Sally nodded. "I brought some."

The woman turned around. A pair of shoes was sticking out from behind a stack of boxes. The woman kicked the shoes and someone cried out.

A boy, younger than Sally, sat up and rubbed his eyes as if he'd been sleeping.

"Get up," the woman said. "Take this… this… what's your name?" she asked Sally.

"Tim," she said.

"Take Tim here to see the Earl."

The boy protested and grumbled as they went out the back door of the tavern. Covering his head with his hands, he ran down a narrow alley as Sally followed. They came out at the end of another dock.

The boy motioned, and Sally followed him up the gangplank of a ship that was moored there. They went below deck and stopped at the door to a cabin.

"Wait now," the boy said. He rapped twice on the door, then waited for a second and rapped three more times. "It's a signal," he explained. "If you go in without it, he'll shoot you."

Sally stared at him. "It's all right, now," the boy said. Sally waited for him to open the door, but the boy said, "You have to go in by yourself. This is as far as I'm allowed."

Sally turned the shiny brass knob and stepped inside. Her mouth dropped open. The cabin was lined with blue velvet wallpaper, shelves holding leather-bound books stamped in gold, and paintings of beautiful country scenes.

She hardly glanced at these, however, for across the room was a slim young man lying on a sofa. He wore a bright blue robe, and red slippers–and he was pointing a flintlock pistol at her.

"Oh, dear," the man said, lowering the pistol. "Would you mind terribly standing just where you

are? Please don't step on the carpet."

Sally looked down. She couldn't help asking, "What kind of carpet is that?"

"Turkish," he said. "A present from the Sultan for a certain favor I did for him. He gave me these slippers too," he said, wagging his feet. "Like them?"

"Are you the Earl?" Sally had imagined that he would be more like a pirate.

"Indeed I am, and I would like to know whom I have to thank for interrupting this fascinating novel I was reading."

Sally looked through the open door, but the boy was gone.

"Not him," said the Earl, snapping his fingers. "Who told you to come to me?"

"Oh. Mr. Franz, in Richmond."

"Ah, Max. I should have guessed. Dear old Max, with his fondness for stray puppies and…." The Earl lifted a small telescope to his eye and pointed it at Sally. "…damsels in distress. You are a damsel, aren't you?"

"Yes," Sally admitted. "And I need quinine."

"Very good," said the Earl, clapping shut his telescope. "Come right to the point. That's the way I like to do business. Spare me the sad story that you must have told Max. How much quinine? A hundred liters?"

"I just need enough for my brother. He has typhus."

"You see? There's the sad story. Well, two ounces, then. No guarantees. No money back if he dies anyway. My price is ten dollars, gold."

Sally's heart sank. "Mr. Franz said the price would be five dollars."

"That was the price before the Battle of Gettysburg. Now the hospitals are full—in Washington and Richmond—and the price is ten dollars. Law of supply and demand, I'm afraid."

"I have some Confederate money," Sally said.

The Earl held up his hand. "I use that for lighting my cigars."

Sally felt tears come to her eyes. To have come all this way… and now, because of this greedy man, not to get the quinine after all. But she wouldn't give him the satisfaction of seeing her cry. "I could send you the rest," she said.

The Earl wasn't listening. He had his telescope aimed at her again. "Is that a silver ring on your finger?" he said in his silky-smooth voice.

She hid her hand behind her back. "It's my mother's," she said.

"Oh, well, then of course you couldn't give it to save your brother's life. Your mother wouldn't like that, would she?"

Slowly, Sally took the ring off her finger.

"Toss it over here, will you?" said the Earl. "Remember the carpet."

She flung it at him, but he caught it neatly in one hand. He examined it, testing its weight. "I'm feeling generous," the Earl said. "I can see you didn't arrive in a carriage. How were you planning to get back to Richmond?"

Sally sighed. She hadn't even thought about that. "Walk, I guess."

"Well, that will take you a week, at least. Rather late for your brother. I happen to be shipping some goods to Yorktown today. You can ride on the wagon with my driver. And I'll give you a hot meal, dry clothes, and a slicker. A cup of tea would do you good. Mine is much better than anything you've drunk lately, I imagine. Can't ask for better than that, can you?"

Yorktown. Maybe, Sally thought, I can sleep at our house. I can think there. Maybe I can borrow a horse from the Mallorys. "All right," she said.

The Earl rang a little bell that sat on a table by the sofa. "Someone will take care of you now," he said. "And if you get back to Richmond, do give my best wishes to Max."

Chapter 13
A Favor Returned

The man who drove the Earl's wagon was wearing the uniform of a Yankee soldier. Sally was surprised but decided not to ask about it. She was dry under the slicker, even though the rain was still pouring down on her. And nestled inside a canvas pack she was carrying was the bottle of quinine that could save Rob's life.

That was all that mattered now. Mama would forgive her, Sally knew, for giving the ring in exchange for the quinine.

They reached the turnoff on the road to Yorktown just as night was falling. "I'll get off here," Sally told the driver. He shrugged and brought the wagon to a halt. She climbed down and headed for the farm where, long ago it seemed, her family had been happy.

Sally knew she could find it in the dark, and at

least the rain seemed to have kept everyone else inside. On the road from the coast, they had passed only a few Yankee soldiers, looking wet and miserable. They had barely glanced at the wagon.

Still, Sally wished that she could see lights from the other houses near theirs. Every one looked empty and abandoned. As she came to the top of the hill that looked down on her family's farm, she tried to remember the night when she and Tim and Nora and Rob had come back from town after dark. Seeing the lamp Mama left in the window, they knew that they would soon be sitting around the fireplace, eating some hot corn muffins with butter melting on them.

She couldn't see anything now. Nothing at all, and that seemed strange, for even at night in the storm, she ought to see something–the familiar outline of the roof and the barn farther back.

When she reached the front gate, Sally understood. It was torn off its hinges and lay on the ground. And up ahead was something that made her heart stop.

She didn't want to look, but her feet carried her forward anyway. Maybe if she got closer she'd find that what she saw wasn't really there.

But when she reached the stone steps at the porch where Gramp liked to sit and read his newspaper, there was nothing at the top of them.

It was all gone. She reached down and picked up a charred piece of wood. The Yankees had burned the house. Only the stone chimney rose above the ashes. As the rain poured down, Sally stood there and cried. She screamed in anger and let the tears run down her face with the rain.

Numbly, she walked down the path to the barn. That had been burned too, and the tobacco shed. Everything.

When she had no more tears to cry, Sally wandered aimlessly through the muddy fields. She couldn't think. She had no idea what to do now. All day she'd been imagining what it would be like to sleep in her own bedroom again. Even in an empty house, she would have felt close to her family and thought of a way to get back to Richmond.

She realized that the rain had stopped pouring on her. She was in the little stand of pines by the stream where she and Tim fished. The branches overhead gave her some shelter from the storm. This was as good a place to stop as any. She brushed away the pine needles under the trees to clear a dry place to lie down.

The next thing she knew, she was dreaming that she had found Jake. He was rubbing her face with his wet muzzle, wanting a carrot. She kept brushing him away, saying, "I haven't got any carrots, Jake. They're all gone. The Earl has them."

She opened her eyes and looked into Jake's. It *was* him, looking down at her. Sally sat up, not quite sure this wasn't still a dream.

"So you ain't dead," came a voice. It wasn't Jake. It was Mattie, the slave girl from the Mallory plantation. She was sitting on Jake's back.

"Guess this horse knows you," Mattie said.

"He's my horse," Sally told her.

"Huh-uh," Mattie said, shaking her head. "Bottom rail on top now."

Sally looked puzzled.

"Don't you know what that means?" Mattie asked. "That's what Old Moses said to Mr. Mallory when the Yankee soldiers got to our plantation and set us free. Old Moses—you met him, remember?

He'd worked for Mr. Mallory ever since he was a little boy. More'n 60 years, old Moses said. And now, he told Mr. Mallory, the bottom rail of the fence got to be on top for once."

Sally remembered Gramp telling her that Lincoln had freed the slaves in the Confederate States last year. But Gramp had said, "Sayin' they're free is easy enough. But settin' them free's another." But the Yankees really had done it.

Sally stood up and brushed the pine needles off her slicker. "So you're free now."

"Free as you are. What're you doing here anyway? Thought you all left when the Yankees were comin'. Are you back to get your gold and jewels?"

"We didn't have any gold or jewels," Sally said.

"I had a ring, but it's gone now."

"Yankees thought you did," said Mattie. "Searched all over for it, I hear. Then they burned everything down when they couldn't find it. 'Course they burned a lot of other places too, just for spite."

"I came back…" Sally began. "Oh, it's too long a story."

"I see you got a pack. That's where you hid the gold and jewels?"

Sally opened the pack and showed Mattie the bottle. "This is medicine for my brother. He's in the hospital at Richmond. He'll die without it. I went down the river to Norfolk to get it. Now I've got to take it back. Won't you let me have Jake?"

"I found him," Mattie said. "Fed him and took care of him. The Yankees said we could keep what we found. 'Course they're gone now, went off to do more fighting. Most of the slaves followed after them, because they figured they'd be free only if there were Yankees around."

"Why didn't you go?" asked Sally.

"Remember I told you 'bout my mamma bein' sold away?"

"Yes."

"Well, I wanted to go find her, but Mr. Mallory wouldn't ever tell me where she'd been sold to. So I thought if the Yankees freed her, wherever she is, she'd come back looking for me. She promised she would. So the only way I'll find her is to wait here."

"So you don't really need Jake."

"Ridin's a lot better'n walkin'. Bottom rail on top now, remember?"

Sally thought. She pulled out the five-dollar gold piece that Mr. Franz had given her. "I'll give you this for Jake. It's all I've got."

Mattie took it, turned it over in her fingers and then handed it back. "I don't need this."

"But you could buy something with it."

Mattie got down from Jake's back and handed

the reins to Sally. "You already gave me something. Remember that honey?"

Sally nodded.

"That was worth more'n any gold to me. I saw what happens to people over gold. When the Yankees came, Miz Mallory brought out all her gold and jewels right quick and said they could have them if they wouldn't burn her house down. So they didn't, but now she's near starving in that big old house, 'cause all her slaves are gone and she don't know how to work. Celia takes her some food sometimes, out of pity."

"What happened to Mr. Mallory?"

"He died right after the Yankees freed his slaves. Can't say I was sorry. No, you can have this horse. If I took your gold, I'd still owe you for the honey. So now we're even. And look at him."

Jake was nodding his head, ready for Sally to take him for a ride.

"This horse knows whose horse he is," said Mattie. "That's good enough for me."

Sally pulled herself onto Jake's back. "Thank you," she told Mattie. "I hope your mamma comes back."

"She will," said Mattie. "Hurry along now. Get that medicine to your brother."

Sally waved and set off toward Richmond.

Chapter 14
Let Me Be in Time

Jake liked the mud. Sally thought it must feel cool and soft to his old feet. Even so, he couldn't move very fast. And by noon he was tired, so she stopped to let him rest.

Even though the rain had stopped, she still hadn't seen very many people along the road. The Yankee soldiers had pulled back from here, but people hadn't returned to their abandoned farms and plantations. In fact, she couldn't recall seeing anybody in more than an hour. It was spooky.

There was a field off to the side of the road that had some turnips growing in it. Sally didn't know if the people who planted them were still here. She pulled a few, and they were large enough to make a meal for Jake. She tried to eat one too, but without being cooked it tasted like a stone.

"Hey, you!" She looked up to see a boy coming

toward her. He was wearing a big black hat that almost covered his face, but the rest of his clothes were too small for him. It would almost have been funny, but he was also pointing a shotgun at Sally.

"I'm sorry," she called. "My horse was hungry, and I didn't think anyone would mind."

"I guess you're a Yankee, then," he said. "That's what they do, just take whatever they want. Don't care about the people who planted them and need them for food."

"I'm not a Yankee," she said. She took off her cap and let her hair fall around her shoulders. The boy lowered his gun, looking sheepish.

"I know what it's like to tend crops," Sally said. "My family had a farm back along the road to Yorktown. Last night I found out that the Yankees burned everything we owned."

"That the truth?" the boy asked. "What happened to your folks?"

"My father and brothers are in the Confederate army. My mother and sister and Gramp are in Richmond."

He nodded. "They just left you here?"

"No. I'm trying to get back there now. My brother Rob is in the hospital, and I've got medicine for him."

"How'd you find out he was there?"

"I was working there."

"You wouldn't know if there was anybody there name of Andrew Carter?"

"No, I don't. There are lots of men there now. They were wounded at Gettysburg."

"Where's that?"

"In Pennsylvania. Didn't you hear about it?"

The boy didn't reply. Close up, Sally could see his face. He was only about ten years old. Sally thought he looked almost as lost as she was. "I guess I might as well tell you," he said finally. "Andrew Carter's my pa. My name's Cal. Cal Carter."

"I'm Sally Bradford." The boy held out his hand, and she shook it.

"See," the boy went on, "Pa went off to the war too. Then there was just me and my brother and sister and Ma. Well, there was some kind of sickness through here. The smallpox, people called it. With the Yankees and the fighting too, most everybody cleared out of these parts."

"Why didn't you leave?"

"Ma got sick. And then my brother. I didn't have no medicine. There wasn't none to get. They both died."

"Oh! That's terrible."

Cal took a deep breath. "I had to bury 'em myself. Nobody'd come near our place 'cause they was afraid of the smallpox. Before Ma died, she made me put up a yellow flag on the house. That's to warn people that there's smallpox inside. Ma told me to get out and take Priss. That's my sister. But I didn't. Since then, we've just been waiting for Pa. I wrote him a letter but he never wrote back."

"So that's why you asked me if he was in the hospital."

Cal nodded. "Priss and I've been trying to get by, but it's hard not knowing if my pa is...." Cal didn't finish, but Sally understood.

"Haven't you got any relatives?" she asked. Why don't you go to Richmond?"

Cal shrugged. "They say there's people starving there. We'd just have to beg. Here, we can grow something, get eggs from the chickens. I shoot rabbits and raccoons when I can. I figure we're better off here."

"But you're too young! How old is your sister?"

"She's eight. But look at you. Riding through here on your horse as if you was going to a church supper. There's desperate people on the road. They'd kill you for your horse, even though he don't look like much. What's your ma think of you being out here?"

"I didn't tell her I was going," Sally admitted.

"So don't tell me I'm too young to be farming.

Priss and I will be all right long as nobody else steals our food."

"I'm sorry," said Sally. "I can give you five dollars for the turnips."

He waved his hand. "Nothing to buy around here. Stores are all empty and shut. You can do me one favor though."

"What's that?"

"If you get to Richmond, try and find out if Andrew Carter's...you know."

"I promise," she said. "I'll find some way to let you know."

"Obliged. And here, I can give you something that will keep you from harm's way."

"I don't want your shotgun."

"Think I'm crazy? No, I'll give you the yellow flag Ma made me put up. I guess Priss and I aren't going to need it. But when people see that, they keep their distance."

He was right. As Sally rode farther down the road, a couple of men came out from behind a rock and called for her to stop. When she waved the yellow flag, it worked better than if she had a gun. The men turned on their heels and ran.

She had to sleep in the woods one more night, but at least the weather had cleared. As she looked at the stars shining overhead, she prayed. Please, please let me be in time.

The next day, Sally passed through the Confederate army lines east of Richmond. The soldiers were startled when they saw her, even though she hid the yellow flag. When she told them her story, they brought her to an officer.

"That horse is about ready to give out, young lady," the officer told her. "Leave him here, and you can ride on to Richmond with a supply wagon."

"I can't leave Jake again," she said. "He won't understand."

"We'll give him the best of care," the officer assured her. "I'll give you a note so you can come back and claim him later."

When Sally saw Jake last, he was contentedly munching some oats in a stall filled with straw. He looked up at her and made the huffing noise that meant he was glad the ride had ended.

It wasn't quite over for Sally, but that afternoon

she got off the supply wagon in front of the hospital. Going inside was almost the hardest part of the trip. What if she was too late? What if Mama...? She'd have to face Mama sometime. It couldn't be worse than what Sally had already been through. Or could it?

Sally went straight to Mrs. Pember's office.

"Sally!" Mrs. Pember exclaimed, staring at her. "Where have you been? Your mother has been–"

"That doesn't matter," Sally said. "Here." She took the bottle from her pack. "This is quinine. I brought it for Rob. Is he all right?"

"He's very ill," Mrs. Pember said. "But this will help. Where did you get it? We could use so much more of it."

Sally shook her head. "I didn't have enough rings for any more."

Mrs. Pember gave her such a strange look that Sally began to laugh. She pressed her hands over her mouth, but couldn't stop. Mrs. Pember made her sit in a soft chair and gave her a glass. "Here. Drink this."

Sally shook her head. "You've got to give the quinine to Rob."

"Drink it!"

Sally's throat felt like fire as the brown liquid went down. She couldn't breathe. But she stopped laughing.

"Wait here," Mrs. Pember said. She left with the quinine.

Sally wanted to follow her, to see Rob, to find Mama. But now that it was over, she felt tireder than she'd ever felt in her life. She didn't think she could move from this chair ever. She closed her eyes.

When she opened them again, the lamp on Mrs. Pember's desk was lit. Outside, it was dark. Sally heard a voice in the corridor outside the office. That was what had awakened her.

It sounded like... but no, it couldn't be. She must have been dreaming again.

And then Papa walked through the door. Wearing his uniform, looking just the way she'd last seen him. No, she thought, not really the same. His hair had gray in it, his arm was in a sling, and there were lines in his face. She couldn't tell if the lines meant he was angry at her.

Right behind him was Mama. And there was no puzzle about the look on *her* face. "Sally Bradford," she said. "Do you have any idea what worry you've caused us?"

"Mama," she said, "I am so sorry, but there wasn't time to ask you."

"Time! You know what I would have done. When we learned from Mr. Franz where you intended to go, I couldn't believe it. What if you...what if...?"

"Mama," Sally said, "that was the same question I asked myself many times. And I remembered what you told me about what ifs."

Mama threw up her hands and turned to Papa. "This is the war," she said. "This is what the war has brought down on us."

"Oh, Mama," said Sally. "Please, please don't talk about the war. People are suffering so much, even worse than us."

"Amen," Papa said. He put his good arm around Sally and gave her a hug. Mama wrapped her arms around them both. "You've probably saved Rob's life," Mama said. "But never, ever do that again!"

Epilogue: 1865

The war was over. The South had lost. Sally had seen Richmond itself in flames. Aunt Jane's house went up in smoke, and Sally's family lived in a tent.

At least Gramp hadn't had to go through that. One morning they found Gramp in his chair. The newspaper on his lap told of another Confederate defeat. They didn't know if that was what killed him.

After Rob got better, he went back to fight some more, and so did Papa. But when General Lee surrendered, there was no more fighting to be done.

No one had heard from Tim in a long time, and they feared the worst. The Bradfords decided to return to their farm, even though Sally told them what to expect.

"This is all we have," Papa said when he saw their ruined farm. "So we have to make the most of it." By now they were used to living in tents, and that would do until they built another house.

Every time Sally went to the creek, she thought of the stormy night she spent under the pines. One day as Sally was coming back with a string of fish, Mattie called to her from the road. A woman Sally had never seen before was with her.

"This is my mamma," Mattie said. "I just wanted to let her see white people working."

"Hush, child," her mamma said. "These are good folks. If you talk like that, somebody will whip you."

"Nobody's ever going to whip me again," Mattie said.

"I'm sure of that," Sally said. "What are you going to do now?"

"Mrs. Mallory's letting ex-slaves farm parts of her land in return for a share of the crop," Mattie said. "I thought we'd try that and maybe save enough to buy some land of our own."

"I'll probably be seeing you often, then," said Sally.

"Whatever happened to your old horse, Jake?" Mattie asked.

"He died," Sally told her. "I left him with some soldiers, and I know they treated him well, but the ride really was too much for him."

"Don't feel bad," said Mattie. "I'll bet he enjoyed taking you on one last ride."

"I hope so," said Sally. "He helped save my brother's life."

"So you're all safe now."

"No," Sally said. "Tim hasn't come home. His name isn't on the list of the dead, but lots of soldiers were never found after the battles."

"It's like me not knowin' where my mamma was," Mattie said. "Hard not knowin'."

"I did help someone else find his father," Sally said. "A boy I met after you let me have Jake. His father was in the hospital where Rob was."

"I'd like to hear all about that ride of yours sometime," Mattie said.

"It takes a long time to tell. Sometimes I wonder how I did it," Sally said.

"People can get through a lot if they have to," Mattie replied. "Maybe your brother will show up one of these days."

Less than a week later, he did, walking down the road, his clothes tattered and the soles of his shoes flapping. Tim had grown a mustache too.

"What took you so long?" she asked, giving him a hug.

"Had to walk all the way," he told her. "You wouldn't believe the things I've seen. Have I got a story to tell you!"

"I'll bet I can match it," she said.

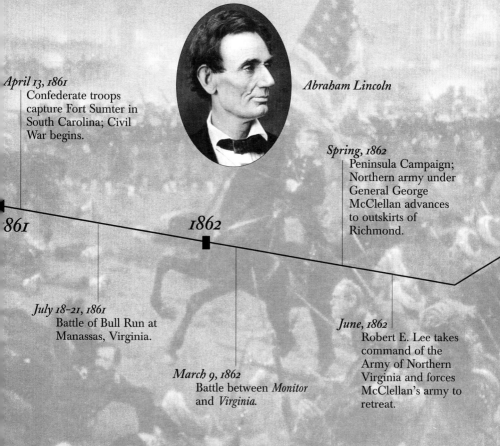

Timeline

This timeline shows the major events of the Civil War. It starts with the fall of Fort Sumter, when President Lincoln ordered the Union Army to put down the "insurrection," or rebellion. It ends four years later with the surrender of General Robert E. Lee to General Ulysses S. Grant.

Abraham Lincoln

April 13, 1861
Confederate troops capture Fort Sumter in South Carolina; Civil War begins.

Spring, 1862
Peninsula Campaign; Northern army under General George McClellan advances to outskirts of Richmond.

1861

1862

July 18-21, 1861
Battle of Bull Run at Manassas, Virginia.

June, 1862
Robert E. Lee takes command of the Army of Northern Virginia and forces McClellan's army to retreat.

March 9, 1862
Battle between *Monitor* and *Virginia*.

Ulysses S. Grant

March, 1864
Ulysses S. Grant is
given command of all
the Union armies.

May, 1863
Battle of
Chancellorsville;
Stonewall Jackson is
killed.

August, 1862
Second Battle of Bull
Run, or Manassas.

1864

September, 1862
Battle of Antietam;
McClellan defeats
Lee.

1863

1865

April 2, 1865
As Grant's forces
approach, the
Confederate govern-
ment leaves Richmond
Fires set by
Confederate troops
spread through the city

July 1–3, 1863
Battle of Gettysburg in
Pennsylvania; Lee
loses one-third of his
army and retreats to
Virginia.

December, 1862
Battle of
Fredericksburg; Lee
prevents the Union
army from crossing
the Rappahannock
River.

April 9, 1865
General Robert E. Lee
surrenders to General
Grant at Appomattox
Court House,
Virginia.

Robert E. Lee

The True Story

Many Southern women kept journals of their experiences during the War Between the States. One of the best known is that that of Mary B. Chesnut, who lived for part of the war in Richmond, Virginia. We have also used Sallie B. Putnam's account, *Richmond During the War,* and the collection *Women of the South in War Times,* compiled by Matthew Page Andrews.

Phoebe Pember was a real person, who published her own book, *A Southern Woman's Story.* She was born Phoebe Yates Levy in Charleston, South Carolina, in 1823. Her prosperous and cultured Jewish parents hired tutors to give Phoebe and her six brothers and sisters a good education.

Phoebe married Thomas Pember, a Boston merchant who moved to Georgia. In the first year of the Civil War, Phoebe's husband died of tuberculosis. Phoebe returned to her parents' home, but decided she must use her talents to serve the Confederacy.

One of Phoebe's friends was the wife of the Confederate Secretary of War. She helped Phoebe obtain the position of matron at Richmond's Chimborazo Hospital. At that time, it was still unusual for women to work in hospitals. At first, the male doctors resented her and tried to make her job more difficult.

However, Phoebe soon began to recruit other women volunteers. They proved able to withstand the terrible sights of wounded and dying soldiers. Phoebe insisted on cleanliness in the rat-infested wards, and got rid of doctors who were incompetent.

During the war, over 76,000 patients were brought to Chimborazo Hospital. Phoebe carried out the herculean task of obtaining food and medicine for them.

After the war, she began to write her memoirs, which were published in 1879. She traveled throughout the United States and Europe, and died in 1913. The United States honored her memory with a postage stamp in 1995.

Phoebe Pember

DATE DUE

NOV 0 1 2001		
11/25		
DEC 3 1 2001		
MAR 0 5 '03		
DEC 1 9 2007		
DEC 1 9 2007		
GAYLORD		PRINTED IN U.S.A.